WILD HORSE KILLERS

Mel Ellis

SCHOLASTIC BOOK SERVICES
New York Toronto London Auckland Sydney Tokyo

ISBN 0-590-30034-2

12 11 10 9 8 7 6 5 4 3 2 1   11   0 1 2 3 4 5/8

Foreword

Once numbering in the millions, the wild horse of the Western plains was driven to near extinction by the middle of the twentieth century. Only through the combined effort of many environmental organizations, and a determined effort by the schoolchildren of America was Congress finally pressured into providing partial protection by eliminating harassment of the wild horse, but only on federal lands.

But no sooner had the remaining nucleus of some fifteen thousand mustangs doubled their number by 1975, than predatory man was clamoring once more for his hide and hooves and flesh.

Even the elk, the deer, and the antelope fared better. To hunt them a man needed a license. And where the wild horse might be rounded up by the thousands for the pet food processing centers, hunters of elk, deer, and antelope usually had to be satisfied with one animal per year.

In the beginning the wild horse was driven back into barren lands by ranchers because it competed with his sheep and cows for grass, though often he picked the best animals to add to his own remuda of riding horses for the great cattle roundups.

Wars too took their toll, and the horse was drafted into the Civil War cavalries of both the North and the South. World War I put a half-million wild horses under saddle, only to have them become casualities to the motorized tank.

Then it was the fox farms clamoring for wild-horse flesh. Then the mink farms. And finally all processing plants in the billion-dollar business of feeding cats and dogs.

The wild horse of the Western plains, for many the American symbol of freedom, is not truly wild. He is a feral animal, an animal once domesticated only to escape back to the wild condition.

America's only true wild horse disappeared from the continent about eight thousand years ago under mysterious conditions — perhaps an epidemic which wiped it out.

Ancestors of today's wild horses were the Spanish Andalusians, a tough, wiry breed brought to the South and the West by Spanish conquistadors. Some of these animals escaped to form the first wild bands. They were called *mesteños* (mustangs) and flourished, their herds increasing even on arid lands.

Few mustangs ever came east of the Mississippi because they did best where the plains were wide and horizons rose from flatlands to mountainous country. Over the hundreds of years many domestic horses from the ranches escaped to add their blood to that of the wild ones. But even to this day, the wiry toughness of those first Andalusians is a characteristic of the mustang.

— M.E.

Part One

1

That night few coyotes celebrated the rising of the moon. Perhaps they knew about the heat which would soon turn the grass bronze and dry up the prairie water holes. Except for the steady beat kept by the crickets, and the muted drone of the electric light plant, it was quiet in the long living room of the white ranch house.

Pace Bradford sat near a floor lamp reading a stock journal. Mrs. Webley, the housekeeper, was fanning herself with a handkerchief and crowding the screen door as if hoping for a breeze. Sandra, her elbows on a windowsill, was looking out at a sky salted with silvery stars. Occasionally bursts of laughter floated up from the bunkhouse where the four hired hands lived.

Otherwise the night seemed waiting. Sandra,

getting up to brush past Mrs. Webley on her way to the porch, wondered what it was that made these backcountry nighttimes seem like intervals of breathlessness, dark interludes of in-between.

At the University of Hammond, where she had just finished her freshman year, nights sparkled with light, laughter, music, and always the raucous roar of traffic. In Hammond people seemed more alive after sunset. Like nocturnal creatures, they came out of classrooms, stores, homes, offices, factories . . . to celebrate the freedom from study and work which the nighttime so luxuriously afforded.

But here at the ranch, in the quiet valley, the nighttime creatures were a slinky, silent tribe — owls on velvet wings, deer soft as moving shadows, pumas on padded paws, cottony jackrabbits with antennae ears questing to catch the first quiver of danger.

Sandra walked across the porch and sat on the steps. She turned to look at the looming blackness of Sawtooth Mountain. Up there little creeks came down to join and form the Sawtooth River, which ran full and strong each spring. All her lifetime she had never tired of exploring the canyons, riding among the tall trees to the timberline where she could turn her horse and look out on the panorama of flatlands below.

It was among these foothills that the cattle came in winter when raging blizzards drove them off the prairie. Here many mule deer lived, and on many a camping trip Sandra had seen the antlered bull elks, sometimes white-bearded goats, an occasional silver-tipped grizzly and the not-so-rare puma stalking cottontails, grouse, and deer.

But if the forested mountain slopes and wooded canyons were a wintertime refuge, it was the rolling prairie which Pace Bradford called his "front lawn." It was the front lawn that fed the grass eaters — his cows and horses. Ecologists might have called it "true prairie," a community of nearly two hundred grasses growing high as a man's ankles in some places and higher than his hips in others. Sometimes it stood rigid and dying in the hot sun. Sometimes it galloped in waves ahead of the high winds. But after the rains its multitude of flowers, mostly tiny blooms, melted into a frenzy of color, predominately blue but shot through with bright reds and yellows, more subtle oranges — a variety of shades, some defying classification.

Sandra turned from the foothills to look out over the prairie. In the light of day riding east, horizon would melt into horizon until the prairie ended and the desert began. That was a place to detour, a rocky, sandy, parched land of armed cactus where horned toads and little lizards lived. It was a treacherous land with barren white plains of alkaline earth, shale slopes of flat desert rock which rattled when you walked, and suddenly, sometimes, castles of rimrock rising for no apparent reason except that they were of tougher stuff and even the oldest and most persistent of architects, the winds of time, had hardly been able to scratch them.

Inevitably, of course, if you rode far enough, once again there would be the foothills, earth mounds covered with trees, one rising higher than the next, on and on — doorsteps to the mountains, the first easy and gradual ascent to towering peaks.

Sandra sighed. She was glad to be home. She loved Mountain Spread. Except tonight she was troubled. In the morning Gerald Deever, the veterinarian, would come, and before he left he would have gelded her stallion.

Then if she could understand the necessity of castrating cattle and hogs to produce better beef and pork, of neutering cats and dogs for any of a variety of reasons, she had argued with Pace Bradford, her father, that Rimrock Red was a horse of such special talents that to impede further physical development, to dampen the fires of a spirit wild and tumultuous as any un-bridled wind, amounted to a sin against creation.

What she hadn't told him—hadn't told any-one — was that she had wanted the red stallion to sire a herd of her own horses. Her daydreams included cruising the prairie on the stallion to select, run down, and rope the most physically perfect wild brood mare she could find, and bring her back to the ranch so a succession of foals might form the nucleus of a herd which could outrun any in the West.

But her father had been adamant. They already had one stallion. Stallions did not make cooperative mounts. They were dangerous. With two stallions on the place there would be no assurance of peace in the horse herd. If in her mind Sandra did not acquiesce, she ceased to argue. Most of her life, perhaps for too long, her father's word had been law.

Following the death of her mother when she was ten, Sandra had moved in the shadow of her father. He had taught her to rope and to ride. From him she had learned to start a campfire with wet wood, build a rainproof lean-to of pine boughs with a small hand ax, milk a cow, brand a steer, help a calf which was having troubles being born, participate in the hot, dusty, grueling drives necessary to get the cattle to the loading pens at the railroad in Three Bends.

Next to her father, whom she worshiped perhaps even more than she loved, horses were the most important living things in her life.

She had gone the gamut, from short-legged and often obstinate little ponies, through the worst and the best mounts in her father's remuda, until a year ago when her fascination came to settle on the fiery stallion she called Rimrock Red.

One of her favorite pastimes, when there were hours to spare, was to ride the red stallion out across the prairie and then race him alongside one or another of the bands of wild horses which lived there.

Then, in a burst of speed, she would close in on the fleeing band until her horse was one of them. But if the stallion, after a breathtaking race, could catch up with the wild ones, she'd rein him back. There wasn't a ranch horse living with the endurance to go the distance with the tough little mustangs.

She thought about the wild horses now as she got up from the porch and walked toward the corral, and she wondered if within her lifetime they would become extinct.

All across the West, with the price of beef and pork soaring, the horse killers had been decimating the herds to provide meat for the pet food producers. Scores of environmental groups had joined forces to try to gain protection for the wild horse. At Hammond University Sandra had joined the American Horse Protection Association, whose purpose was to flood the halls of Congress, the schools, and the state capitols with literature appealing for complete protection for all wild horses.

It had never occurred to her to worry about her "own" wild horses, the few scattered bands in the valley where Mountain Spread cattle grazed. The horse killers had been concentrating their efforts where the wild horse was more populous and might be gathered in by the hundreds in stampedes in which helicopters and airplanes played a major role.

Here on the prairie between Sawtooth Mountain and the desert, the entire wild horse population consisted of perhaps three or four bands totaling not more than a hundred head, hardly enough — or so she thought — to tempt the horse killers.

Nearing the corral, Rimrock Red must have scented her because he nickered. She walked to the gate, called softly, and then his head came across the bars and he playfully nuzzled her shoulder, nipping her shirt lightly with his teeth. She rubbed his soft muzzle, brushed her cheek against his nose and then, turning, started back toward the house.

The coyotes had started up. But once again the heat seemed too much for them, and the wailing petered out and trailed off to a whimper — then nothing. One of the hounds tied down in back of the barn bayed briefly, and somewhere out on the prairie a steer bawled. Then, except for the crickets and the hum of the light plant, it was silent as she went quietly up the porch steps and through the door.

The living room was empty. Turning out the light, she went upstairs. She thought again about Deever and the stallion and the morning. With her sleep came sadness. There was no point in dreaming now about red foals sired by a red stallion. It was just not going to happen.

2

Next morning Sandra did not go down for breakfast. She heard the clatter of dishes, the voices of the hired hands, the almost fragile voice of Mrs. Webley urging one more flapjack, one more cup of coffee on the men.

Mrs. Welbley had come to the ranch shortly after the death of Sandra's mother. Her coming had been a thing as gentle and unobstrusive as a ray of morning sun creeping across a rug. At once she had become a fixture, always in the background, hardly noticed — except when Pace Bradford forgot that a small girl needed more from a parent than a lecture on how never to flinch when pulling the trigger of a rifle. Then Mrs. Webley would interrupt. It would be only with raised eyebrows, or a kindly yet intense look. But Pace Bradford would put the rifle back in the gun rack and, looking embarrassed, go stomping out of the house. Or, when the time came, she would suggest — in an offhand, quiet way — that Sandra had outgrown her clothes and it was time for a Three Bends shopping trip.

Sandra sat up in bed now. A car had come into the yard. That would be Gerald Deever. From below she heard her father's voice, "He's here. Let's get going." Then there was the sound of chairs being moved, of hard riding-boot heels on the bare floor between the scattered rugs, the sound of the screen door slamming.

Sandra threw back the sheet and went to the window. Deever's white omnibus, gray with prairie dust, was down by the corral. It was a mobile medical unit, complete with refrigeration for more fragile drugs.

While she watched, three of the hands — George, Dyke, and Williams — went on down to the barn. The other, Chase Long, accompanied her father to greet Deever.

Four horses, including Red, were in the pole corral. Deever was eyeing them as he got into and then buttoned the front of the white coat which fell to his boot tops.

Sandra turned away. She would not watch. Though she preferred her shower at the end of the sometimes long, dusty and sweaty days, she decided to take one now.

But even the sounds of the shower could not drown out the shouts of the men, the sometimes anguished nickering of a horse. Nevertheless she soaped deliberately and dried thoroughly before getting into jeans and a shirt. As she finished twisting her long black hair into two tight braids, she couldn't help herself any longer. She went to the window, and sinking to the floor so her chin rested on the sill, looked out through the narrow aperture between the white curtains.

At once she saw that three of the four horses in the corral had already been gelded. Her horse, shimmering in the slanting rays of the rising sun, had thus far escaped Long's rope, and now stood at the far end of the corral, front legs braced and nostrils quivering.

One of the other horses, a bay, had not yet recovered from the anesthetic. He was on the ground, sides heaving. The other two, a white and a pale roan, stood off to the side on wobbly legs, heads still hanging, saliva dripping from foaming muzzles.

Sandra's fingers bit into the windowsill as Long came within roping range of her horse. Then the breath which she had been holding was expelled in a triumphant snort as the horse once again evaded the noose and charged to send the ranch hand climbing for the safety of the top pole of the corral.

Pace Bradford, who had been standing by the gate, said, "Damn!" Then to Long he added, "Wait, I'll get Sandra. He'll stand for her."

Bradford crossed the dusty yard and then Sandra heard his boots on the steps. "Sandra?" he called quietly, at first. Then, "Sandra!"

She heard his boots coming up the steps, then his knock on the door. "Come in," Sandra said. Pace Bradford looked annoyed.

"Unless you help, that horse'll get hurt," the father said.

Sandra stared at her father. "Not if you don't put a rope on him."

Pace Bradford's eyes, black as Sandra's, snapped back. "We're not going to get into that again," he said.

Sandra wanted to say, "Then you go and do your own dirty work," but she checked herself.

"For a woman in college, you're not showing good sense," Pace said.

He turned to go, then turned back again. "Sandra," he said, "we're going to castrate that horse one way or another. Now if you want to make it easy on the animal you'll come down and catch and hold him so the vet can give him a shot. If you don't, he might get his damn neck broken."

With that he left. Sandra could hear his boots on the stairs, and the front screen door creak open and slam shut. She went to the window and watched him cross the yard to where Long and Deever waited.

The red horse was as far from the men as he could get, his haunches pressed against the poles of the corral, his head high now with ears erect for the first sound of danger, nostrils flared for the first odor of danger, and brown eyes moving for the first sight of danger.

He was a wild horse, wild as any of the wild ones which still roamed the prairie. He was rebellious too, hating the touch of any hand except hers, and tolerating hers only because she had helped him through the abrasive weeks of weaning with an occasional bottle feeding to ease his loss, and then gentled him with sugar

13

and apples so that he permitted the bit in his mouth when she was on his back.

But now they were going to quench some of the fire. Then if at some later date in a fractious moment he might rear and paw the air and scream about how he was swift and strong, it would only be a momentary reminder of a great stallion who had seen his masculinity spilled out on the gray dust in the pole corral.

Pace Bradford turned to Chase Long. "Go get him!"

The horse had lowered his head, eyes intent on the man with the rope. As the rope came closer and closer and then went snaking out, the horse threw up his head and reared. The loop caught a front hoof, pulled tight around the fetlock, and the horse was off with a burst of speed. When he came to the end of the rope, he went somersaulting, and the wind went out of him with an explosive grunt.

"Now!" Bradford shouted, hurrying toward the horse. But Long was on his belly, put flat and dragged when the rope went tight.

Before Bradford could get to the animal, the horse suddenly was up again. With the rope trailing from the front leg, he went bucking, rearing and twisting around the corral.

"You'll kill him!" The girl at the window screamed.

"WAIT!" she shouted, and darted down the stairs.

3

Tail arched, ears forward, nostrils flared, the red horse stood at the far end of the corral quivering. Sandra's voice had been sharp and commanding.

"WAIT!" she had repeated as she ran. "You'll kill him," she cried at the corral gate. Then, as if in surrender, "I'll hold him for you."

The three men eyed one another guiltily.

Sandra ducked under the poles and entered the corral. "Okay, Red. Okay," she clucked soothingly. At the sound of her voice the horse threw back his head and whinnied. "Good horse," she said, moving smoothly and slowly toward him.

When she was directly in front of the stallion she stopped. "Come on, Red. Come on," trying to get the horse to come to her. Though he had stopped quivering and had lowered his tail, he stood his ground.

"Come on, Red. Good horse. Come on, boy." Always before it had been the stallion's habit to walk up to her to have his forehead scratched. Now he held back as if he also distrusted her.

"He knows," she said, turning to the three men. "He knows. He can smell it. The blood. Everything."

The three men said nothing. Chase Long and the girl's father had climbed to the top rail of the corral and sat there. The veterinarian, his long white coat spotted with blood, was sucking curare from a vial into a syringe. Up at the house the housekeeper, Cleta Webley, stood watching through the screen door.

Sandra turned back to the horse. "You going to stand for me?" she asked. Then she moved slowly forward again. The horse's tail came up, arched again, and the nostrils flared as he tossed his head from side to side, rippling the mane like running fire.

"Now. Now," Sandra cautioned. Once again the stallion whinnied. Once again Sandra attempted to get the horse to submit voluntarily. "Come on, boy. Come on, Red," she said, holding out a hand. The stallion took a step, shook his head and rolled his eyes until the whites showed. "Easy, boy. We won't hurt you," she said. But that was a lie. They were going to hurt him. They were going to shove a needle through his glossy hide, inject curare.

Sandra turned to the men as if to plead once again for this bit of surgery to be called off. She stood sideways to the horse looking to where the veterinarian stood, where Mrs. Webley had come out onto the porch, where her father and Chase Long sat.

The obstinate tilt of her father's head convinced her that if she didn't get on with the job, the men would do it in a considerably more brutal manner.

Turning back to the horse once more she urged, "Come on, Red. Come on." And this time the horse stepped forward. Carefully she put up a hand and caressed his neck. Then with the other hand she loosed the rope he had been dragging, and pulling it down over the fetlock, dropped it in the dust. Then she took the stallion by the halter and began to lead him across the corral to where the veterinarian waited.

As they approached Gerald Deever, the horse jerked his head high and began to prance away at an angle. "Don't anybody move," Sandra cautioned, stopping and talking to the horse as if to reassure him.

When he had quieted Sandra said, "Don't walk to me, Mr. Deever. You let me bring him to you. Just stand still."

Clucking softly then, she leaned a little and once more the horse began prancing. She let him prance as she moved until she was standing beside the veterinarian. Then when the stallion shied away from the man Sandra held his head so that with one step Gerald Deever was standing alongside the animal's neck.

At the touch of the vet's hand on his neck, the red stallion quivered from nostrils to fetlocks.

Syringe poised, the veterinarian raised his right hand, ready to send the knockout fluid racing through the horse's bloodstream to hit the nerves, paralyze and bring him to his knees, and then all the way over unconscious.

After that it wouldn't take long. Sandra knew. Gerald Deever would kneel and his hands would dart swiftly between the horse's hind legs. The scalpel would slice once, twice, three times, and then a few more shorter, quicker, darting cuts . . . and it would be over.

In a few minutes the horse would stir, gaze around bewildered, raise his forelegs, collapse, raise again, and then — only a little blood staining each leg — leap erect only to go crashing back down.

Sandra wanted to turn away, but she felt the eyes of her father. She felt the eyes of Chase Long, Mrs. Webley. So she set her face into rigid lines, glued her eyes on the shiny needle, held her breath, and made a tight first of her mind.

The veterinarian's long fingers moved expertly across the glistening hide of the horse's neck, found what they were looking for, and then the needle came forward and with a fluid motion went plunging into an artery.

Red's head went back. His nostrils dilated. His eyes rolled. And then he reared, yanking the girl from her feet and dislodging the needle. Gerald Deever made a grab for the horse's halter, missed and fell, and Red's hooves came down inches from his head.

Pace Bradford and his hired hand jumped

down and started forward, further startling the horse, who reared again, taking Sandra into the air.

"Whoa there! Whoa there!" Pace shouted, trying to get a hand on the halter.

The veterinarian, who had rolled clear of the flailing hooves, was on his knees watching. "Get back," Sandra warned. "Get back! You're only frightening him!"

But her warning came too late. The red horse bolted, Sandra was dragged a few feet before she let go of the halter, and then he hit the side of the corral, and there was the sound of poles snapping as he crashed through to freedom.

Twenty, thirty feet, and then Sandra, seated in the dust, saw him stumble, regain his balance, then stumble again.

"He's hurt!" she cried out.

No sooner had she said it than the red horse went all the way down to his knees, sending up a dust cloud as he plowed the ground.

Sandra was on her feet running. But up ahead the horse recovered and was again galloping toward the creek and a colony of cottonwoods.

Where a lone cottonwood stood like a sentinel separated from the other trees, the horse, as though blind, rammed a shoulder hard against the trunk of the tree, recoiled, started forward, and hit the tree again.

"Red! Red!" Sandra shouted.

Then the horse, almost as if spurred, charged again and sliding past the tree came swiftly to the creek and when he went down the next time it was in a shower of water.

They were all in pursuit now, all except the veterinarian.

Red, back on his feet, glanced around to see the people hurrying toward him. Then he turned, and running in the water, went upstream to disappear among the trees. By the time his pursuers reached the creek bank there was neither sight nor sound of him.

They stood quietly then, Sandra and the men, on the banks of Rushing Creek looking upstream. The father put a hand on his daughter's shoulder, but she shrugged it off. Without a word then, they all turned and walked back to the field, where Deever was standing at the break in the corral lest the other three horses, now fully recovered from the doses of curare, escape.

"Is he hurt?" Sandra managed to ask, looking into the veterinarian's face.

Deever shook his head. "No. Before he threw the needle he got a minute dose of curare. It must have been just enough to numb him."

"Will he be all right?" Sandra asked.

Deever nodded. "It will pass in minutes."

Sandra looked at her father. "I think I'll follow, see if I can catch him."

"Why don't you just wait?" Pace said. "Likely he'll come back of his own accord."

"I don't think so," Sandra said.

"Well, okay."

Sandra started walking toward the trees. The veterinarian went to his bus. Bradford and Chase went to the fence and began making temporary repairs. Mrs. Webley went back into the house.

Two hundred yards up the creek, the girl found where the horse had left the water. She followed his tracks across a low spot, lost them in the brush, found them again where he had crossed a dusty glade. Then the ground lifted precipitously on its way to mountain peaks and the terrain was a jumble of rocks. Further trailing was impossible, and Sandra turned back. She would wait. One day anyway. Then if he did not come back she would go looking for him.

4

The following day Sandra left the ranch at daybreak on a leggy buckskin gelding her father
had named Step-And-A-Half. She followed the
creek, stopping often to listen and to search the
ground for hoof prints.

The foothills were as familiar to her as the
pattern in her bedroom rug. She knew all the
larger rock outcroppings, every canyon, every
rill, even most of the biggest and most elderly of
the towering trees. She knew them from child-
hood, from the time her mother died and her
father had begun packing her around, first on
the back of his saddle or beside him in a jeep.

Sandra followed the creek up into the foothills. She crossed a grizzly track and watched
Step-And-A-Half's ears to see if the bear might

be in the vicinity. But the spoor was old and the horse exhibited no apprehension. At a marshy inlet which fingered away from the creek, she found the young stallion's trail in the soft ground. He was headed downhill toward the prairie.

That made sense. Grazing was poor beneath the trees. What vegetation grew in the forest understory was tough and fibrous, suited to such browers as elk or deer. The stallion would browse on the woody undergrowth if that became necessary, but if there was prairie grass, he would gravitate to it.

Sandra looked around. The thick bed of needles beneath the ponderosa pines was too resilient to retain an impression, and she lost the horse's track. So she headed directly toward the timberline where prairie crept up the slope to meet the trees, and rode out of the shade onto the flatlands, where the sun was directly overhead.

The heat was unbearable. She was about to move out of its range, back to the fringe of forest where she would be in the shade, when a far-off, thin wailing brought her abruptly erect in the saddle. If she hadn't been almost twenty miles from the city of Three Bends, she would have sworn the noise was coming from a siren.

Turning Step-And-A-Half, she spotted what had to be a dust cloud and the source of the sound. At first she didn't notice the airplane. Then it materialized, looking like a circling fly on the pale blue, paper-like horizon. Except what airplane, she wondered, made a noise like a siren?

She slouched in the saddle to take the tension off her leg muscles, and debated whether to investigate the plane and the dust cloud or ride the fringe of the forest for some sign of her horse.

In the end curiosity won out, and she started off at a steady lope to intersect the dust cloud. She hadn't gone far when she saw the reason for dust; a stampeding herd of cattle. But what fool would herd his cows with an airplane equipped with a siren? And then too, what cattle used this particular piece of range other than those of her father?

Sandra leaned forward for a better look. At the shift in weight Step-And-A-Half broke into a ground-consuming gallop. For a time Sandra kept her eyes on the ground watching for prairie-dog holes. When she next looked up the dust cloud was close enough so that she could get glimpses of the galloping animals. The airplane was not driving cattle, but herding horses!

But whose horses? Then it all became clear. The plane, and now she could also see a jeep, was pushing a herd of wild horses toward Three Bends. From there, she was sure the animals would be freighted to eastern pet food processing centers.

Sandra found it hard to believe that the horse killers would invade her valley. She didn't think there were enough wild horses there for them to bother with. Likely it was some local group, but then juggling figures in her head even as she rode, she was surprised when she realized that even a catch of one hundred horses at seven cents the pound made for a financial grab of some seven thousand dollars.

Sandra slowed Step-And-A-Half to a walk. It was a killing pace the stampede had been setting, and she had no intention of riding a good horse into the ground. She was about to swing her horse's head toward home when, like a terrifying streak of white lightning, it occurred to her that Red might have joined the wild ones and that he was at this instant being driven to his death.

She swung her mount around and started at breakneck speed to try to intercept the drive. Suddenly she changed her mind. Her best bet, she realized, was to try to intercept the herd at Three Bends. So she turned abruptly and headed for home. She let Step-And-A-Half have his head, and he lived up to his name, covering the ground with gazellelike bounds that put the wind singing in her ears.

She ran the horse hard for a half mile, and then pulled him back to a less heartbreaking canter, lest the pace kill him. Jackrabbits spurted out of their way, and on a rise a small band of seven antelope went down a shallow draw, their white rump patches flashing the danger they felt.

She was home in half an hour. Step-And-A-Half was lathering at the muzzle, and a rime of foam had formed across his chest. Chase Long came running when he saw her gallop into the yard. She was on the ground in a flash. Then, dropping the reins, she said, "Cool him out, will you, Chase? Walk him down. I've got to get to town."

Running, she headed for the old pickup truck which stood beneath a clump of cottonwoods. By the time she was back of the wheel, Chase Long had found his tongue. "What's up?" he shouted.

"Wild horse roundup," she called back over her shoulder, as the pickup truck rattled out onto the dusty, winding road. "They might have Red!" she shouted, above the clatter of the engine.

At the wooden bridge which spanned Sawtooth River, the truck seemed about ready to scatter parts out across the water. But she kept the throttle depressed and bounced off the bridge onto the velvety dust tracks, and brought the old truck rattling and roaring to where the blacktop road led to Three Bends.

Sixty was as fast as the old truck would go, so she kept the needle of the speedometer there, careening around two huge, semi-trailer trucks, scattering a small flock of crows dining on a road-killed jackrabbit, narrowly missing a stray steer, only easing up at the adobe huts and the clots of children at play.

At thirty miles an hour she crossed the Sawtooth River, which made three bends around the city to give it its name, and then drove down Mesquite Boulevard past the four-story bank building, bounced across the railroad tracks, crossed the river once again and was soon enveloped by a maze of corrals the railroad maintained as holding pens for cattle awaiting shipment.

At the far northwestern edge of the corrals,

many of which held white-faced cattle, she stopped by a loading dock. Jumping up on the dock, she shaded her eyes and looked out across the prairie.

She was on time. Up ahead, a thin trail of dust marked the approaching herd. The horses were no longer running, but were strung out in a long line. Gone was the airplane, but a second jeep had joined the first. Together the two autos were herding the band of wild horses to their doom.

5

Sandra shuddered at the sight. A long line of staggering, glassy-eyed horses, lathered with foam, their nostrils red with blood from tortured lungs, came with hanging heads, ghosts of a once proud and free band that down through the years had defied the icy blasts of blizzards, the onslaughts of such summer suns as blackened their tongues, living sometimes on nothing less than raw courage.

Now whipped to within an inch of their lives, they stumbled drunkenly, falling to their knees, rising, standing on braced legs, heads hanging to the ground, moving only at the insistence of a jeep horn, or staggering forward only when jolted by the jeep itself.

Two weanlings, both with red marks where rifle bullets had entered their foreheads, were drapped across a jeep's back seat, long tongues hanging from between bared teeth — youngsters that hadn't made it, destined for some local freezer.

Sandra looked over the horses. Red was *not* among them, but her concern for her own horse in the face of such bestiality seemed suddenly inconsequential. Her senses stumbled.

The brutality, the savagery, was incomprehensible. Sandra could only grope numbly for answers. Why? For what? Seven cents the pound? Maybe twelve or fifteen cents for those young enough for human consumption? Seventy dollars the head? At the most, a hundred dollars a horse?

She turned away as a corral gate swung wide, and the first horse, a big gangly paint, moved in. One by one the others followed until they were standing huddled in their common misery, eyes fixed and staring, looking strangely like dead horses which had not had the good grace to lie down to do their dying.

"Don't water them until they've cooled out. Might kill them," one of the men said.

The sound of the man's voice, the absence of even a trace of compassion, was like a match to the fuse of Sandra's indignation. Her anger flared as she turned to look at the men standing around one of the jeeps drinking cans of beer from a portable cooler.

"Damn!" she said. And then like quick explosions: "Damn you! Damn you! Damn you!"

The men turned. They were silent, holding their beer cans at chin level, as if surprised by the flood of her anger.

Sandra couldn't return their looks. Tears came instead. She would have liked to hurl curses, to beat up on them.

One of the men laughed self-consciously. Then they all laughed. Frustrated, Sandra turned and walked away, crying. She could hear their conversation.

"How many did we get?" one asked.

"About thirty. Thirty-two with the two foals we had to shoot."

"That's a good day's haul, about three thousand bucks," another said.

"How many you think are in the valley?"

"At least a hundred. Maybe two hundred," someone answered.

"Jeeze! We could wind up with seven, maybe ten thousand dollars."

They were silent again. There was the sound of beer cans popping open.

Sandra crossed and jumped from the loading dock and the dust spurted. Then she ran over to the old truck, and with the engine wheezing began the trek back to Mountain Spread.

She had come only to save one horse, hers, but now as she drove she wondered if there might not be some way to save at least some of the others.

6

Sandra's first thought on getting back to the ranch was to seek out her father and try to relieve her troubled mind by telling him about the tragic episode. But that had not been the way of things since her mother's death.

On the ranch, when a thing was done it was done, and if you had to shoot a steer because it was far gone from an attack of screwworm, you shot it, left the carcass for the efficient buzzards and moved along, onto the next endless succession of jobs that needed doing.

For a moment she contemplated seeking sympathy from Mrs. Webley, sitting in the closeness of the comfortable kitchen and talking so some of the bitterness might be diluted merely by sharing it with another person.

In the end she did neither. Though her schedule called for saddle-soaping all the leathery parts of the equipment in the tack room, she walked instead to the creek where Red had stumbled in flight, and sitting beneath the shade of a cottonwood, stared at the crystal current until she was mesmerized by the flow of water.

Then she got up and walked, spent what remained of the afternoon formulating and discarding one plan after another for saving the rest of the valley's wild horses from the killers.

But when the sun began lowering out where the desert began, and she stood at the prairie edge looking at the white-faced cattle grazing there, the only thing she had decided on for certain was that she had to find Rimrock before he too became caught up in the web and was stampeded along with some other wild band on the journey to some eastern slaughterhouse.

That Red would join a band of wild horses seemed reasonably certain. He was coming into that first vigor which sent every stallion, domestic or wild, looking for mares. It was as inevitable as the flowering of each spring.

The supper bell finally interrupted her musing, turned her toward the ranch. She composed herself as she took her place at the table.

Outside the sun had almost set. The light slanted through the western windows to spread an unnatural, almost hallowed light among the five men and two women sitting at the supper table.

Usually supper was a festive time, the only time of the day when all seven were together. The four ranch hands — sometimes there were only two, depending upon the seasons — always had interesting sidelights on the day's activities, little nuggets of excitement about a belligerent bull, a lost calf, or the tale of how a squirrel had carried her naked offspring from the bole of one tree to the bole of another. Pace Bradford, usually mellowed by his two glasses of homemade wine, reminisced sometimes of the days when he and his young bride moved into a tarpaper shack to start working to build what was now Mountain Spread.

This night, however, they all seemed to sense that something was different, and even before they had lifted their heads following the brief words of grace which Mrs. Webley always insisted upon, Sandra's resolve to remain calm weakened, and the dam which she thought she had built to stem her emotions began to crumble, and tears began to well up in her eyes.

"How could they do such a terrible thing?" The words came unbidden, like a flood of water.

Everyone, of course, stopped eating to look at her. "They drove them with airplanes and jeeps. It was horrible!"

"What is it?" her father asked.

Without taking her eyes from her plate, she told them, and now her composure surprised even herself. After that first gush of emotion, the words came quietly and there was no quaver even of indignation as she related in an orderly fashion how she had taken the truck to Three Bends and saw the hapless band of animals come stringing in off the prairie to huddle in the corral, a mass of mutilated horseflesh.

It was the recital of a woman who had grown

up surrounded by the endless succession of birth and death which is a routine of ranch life. She ended by saying, "But they didn't have Red. Thank God, they didn't have Red."

When she looked up, she knew they all understood. She knew she would not have to put into words the anger and frustration. And then the frustration, which was as physical and hurtful and choking as a lungful of smoke, dissipated, and two tears signaled the relief she suddenly felt.

For a while then they all ate in silence. Pace Bradford was the first to speak. "Just remember," he said, as though he thought it necessary, "that all men aren't cruel."

Sandra poked at the food on her plate. Then she looked at him. "But how," she asked, "can you explain men like that?"

Pace looked disturbed, then the frown on his face disappeared, and he said, "I suppose I explain them like I explain tornadoes, cloudbursts, lightning . . . which really isn't any explanation at all."

Sandra took a different tack: "You know they'll try to get all the horses in the valley." Pace nodded. "But isn't there something we can do?" Sandra asked.

Pace ran his hand over his face. "My guess is these are the usual bunch of toughs who hang around Three Bends trying to scratch up beer money. With the price of horseflesh what it is, they'd have little trouble borrowing or renting jeeps and a plane. We might report it to the sheriff, have the men arrested for cruelty to animals. They might all be fined. But tomorrow they'd be right out running horses again because the profits are large enough to pay any number of fines."

"If only we could get those horses onto federal lands," Sandra said, "they'd be safe."

"How's that!" Pace asked.

"There is a law against the harassment and capture of horses on all federal lands."

"But there are no federal lands in the valley," Pace said.

Sandra was silent for a few moments. Then she asked, "Where are the nearest federal lands?"

Pace frowned, indicating he didn't know. Chase Long, youngest of the ranch hands, answered, "Rantan. Rantan Reservation. All federal land. Maybe two hundred, maybe three hundred miles straight west."

Sandra's face brightened. "Maybe we could round up the scattered herds, drive them to Rantan."

Pace looked irritated, then he laughed. "You're crazy. You're absolutely crazy. You'd have to cross the desert and mountains high enough to discourage a goat."

"Maybe we could freight them there," Sandra said.

"There's not a railroad within a hundred miles of Rantan," Long said.

"Still, there's got to be a way," Sandra said as much to herself as to anybody.

"Better forget it, Sandra," Pace said. "Anyway there likely aren't more than a hundred wild horses in the valley. You'd best forget it."

But Sandra knew she could never forget it. One horse or a hundred, such brutality was beyond comprehension. And to think they might be back, that they almost surely would be back — she shuddered, pushed back her plate, and left the table.

Her father got up when she opened the screen door and stepped out onto the porch. Pace followed. "Is Red out on the prairie?" he asked. When the girl said nothing, Pace asked again, "Is Red out there?"

The girl nodded. "I'm sure he is. His tracks were headed in that direction. Since he hasn't come back, I have to assume that he is."

"You going after him?"

Again the girl nodded.

For a long, long moment the father was silent. Then he said quietly so only she could hear, "Well, good luck. But please, please be careful."

7

Sandra spent an almost sleepless night, and began her search at dawn. She rode hard, stopping on every rise, every hillock to scan the horizon with binoculars.

She saw coyotes, desert foxes, jackrabbits, and prairie dogs, a band of antelope, and the ever present buzzards — silent, hovering birds keeping the death watch — but it wasn't until late in the afternoon that she saw Rimrock Red.

The sun was already in the west, a white-hot orb presaging a torrid summer, when the red stallion suddenly appeared on a sloping ridge. She put the glasses on him and saw at once that he was agitated.

Slouching in the saddle, she braced an elbow

on the pommel to steady the binoculars for a better view of the horse. As she watched she saw him rear and cleave the air with his front hooves. His lips were drawn back over bared teeth, and though he was too far away for her to hear his scream, she knew that he was challenging some unseen enemy.

Then in a typical show of bravado, he began a swift circular trot — neck arched, tail held high, nostrils flared, hooves chopping to send puffs of dust up from among the prairie flowers.

Putting the glasses back in the case, Sandra kneed Step-And-A-Half forward in a swift lope, but before she'd covered half the distance to where the stallion was cavorting, she brought her mount to an abrupt stop when a string of horses came straggling up out of the shallow draw.

Raising the glasses again, she saw that the horses were led by a huge, gangly, hammer-headed mare of multiple spots. Bringing up the rear was a white muscled stallion prodding reluctant mares, some with weanlings, into keeping the pace. It was the white stallion which had brought Rimrock's blood to a boil. Even as she watched, the red stallion dashed in and cut a mare out of the little herd and started her off at a tangent.

Nipping the mare to greater speed, Rimrock never saw the white stallion bearing down on him until he was suddenly shouldered so hard in a sidelong charge that he went to his knees. By the time he was back up, and by the time the dust had settled, the mare was back in the herd and the white stallion was pressing his band so hard they came together in a crush up against the lead mare's flanks to send her into a wild gallop.

Sandra could not help but smile as she saw Rimrock shake himself as if to be rid of the humiliation of going down without getting in a single kick. He stood for several seconds, almost as if contemplating the wisdom of further challenging the white stallion's right to such a wealth of mares.

The pace of the herd slowed almost as abruptly as it had quickened. Then with the gangly mare leading the way east toward the foothills, and the white stallion turning often to stamp and neigh a warning to Rimrock, the herd passed slowly across in front of Sandra with her stallion trailing at a discreet distance.

Sandra looked at her watch. In three hours it would be dark. If she put a rope on Rimrock now, she might get within sight of the ranch before total darkness enveloped the prairie.

Casing the binoculars, looking to the lasso and then pulling down the brim of her hat to shade out the lowering sun, she kneed Step-And-A-Half in an easy lope to intercept the moving band of wild horses.

At once the lead mare saw her coming and whistled and broke into a canter. The white stallion, forgetting about Rimrock, pressed the band of some twenty mares and younger horses of varying sizes into the tireless lope which once made the wiry, wild mustang the favorite all-around mount of the old-time cattlemen who had to make the historic overland drives to shipping railheads.

Rimrock's stride lengthened to keep the herd within mare-stealing distance, and there they were then, strung out loosely across the grassy prairie. The thread of dust being raised by the hurrying horses was also spotted from above by a man in a small plane. Banking sharply, he nosed the plane east to intercept the herd.

Sandra never saw or heard the airplane until it was overhead. She had whistled piercingly, hoping that this customary greeting would turn Rimrock from his quest of mares so she might ride to within easy roping distance and lead the stallion back to the ranch.

The whistle, however, provoked the horses to greater speed until at last Sandra found herself bending into the wind with Step-And-A-Half going at a dead gallop. It was at the very height of the chase that the drone of the airplane penetrated the sound of hammering hooves and the whistling wind. Sandra pulled up at once, slowed Step-And-A-Half to a walk.

The plane came low then, dipped its wings as though greeting a compatriot in this game of hounding wild horses. Sandra realized at once that the pilot had no idea who she was, and had probably decided she was one of the local ranchers intent on roping one or another of the herd to add to his remuda.

Obligingly then, the pilot put his plane between the horses and the protection of the trees which marked the foothills, and turned the band out and back toward open country.

Sandra went immediately into action. Pushing her horse she managed to turn the herd back toward the trees as the airplane, with what seemed like an angry snarl, swooped low and began a wide turn to turn the herd once more, angle it away from the protection of the trees.

Sandra rode hard then, pushing Rimrock and the rest of the herd with shrill whoops and wild abandon toward the cottonwoods which marked the forest fringe. As if sensing her intent, the pilot turned on his siren, and then in a low, screaming swoop once again turned the bewildered herd away from the trees.

But the girl had the advantage. There was no way the airplane could execute the quick turns and maneuvers of a horse. The plane might panic the herd into turning away from the trees, but by the time it could gain altitude again for a turn and another sweep, Sandra had pushed the band a quarter mile closer to safety.

Still it was a grueling, dust-eating, dangerous battle. The screaming machine swept so low its undercarriage sometimes grazed the prairie grasses, and Sandra whipped her mount to such flurries of speed as sometimes put her right among the stampeding horses.

The pilot gave up first. With one last daring dive, a gesture in futility, Sandra was caught in such a blast of prop wash she was almost swept from her saddle. Then the plane climbed and after a lazy circle, as though to mark the spot, flew west to become a pinprick against the blue, and then nothing.

Sandra slowed her horse to a walk. Shortly

then the tired herd was walking, straggling in a long, loose line toward the trees. Sandra, instead of feeling triumphant, was frightened by a deep feeling of foreboding. She knew tomorrow the plane would be back. No longer did it matter that she bring Rimrock in this night. Now it was the safety of all the horses which mattered.

8

All yard lights were blazing at Mountain Spread when Sandra, wearied, rode in on an even wearier horse. The crickets had been celebrating darkness for the better part of an hour when the ranch hands poured from the bunkhouse and Pace Bradford and Mrs. Webley came hurrying off the ranch house porch at the sound of Step-And-A-Half's shrill neigh of hunger and thirst.

Everyone began to question Sandra at once. Her father took her mount's bridle. Sandra slid off and stood swaying for a moment.

Chase Long stepped toward her. She motioned him back, and after a few tentative steps, said, "Well, Red's joined up with one of the bands of wild horses, and would you believe it? The horse killers are after them already!"

After a hot bath and while she sat in the living room sipping a bowl of hot soup, Sandra's father announced, "Well, okay. We'll all go out tomorrow to get him."

Sandra put down her soup spoon and looked at her father. Then she looked at the four ranch hands and Mrs. Webley, all of whom had gathered around her. Then she asked, "What about the other horses?"

For a moment there was silence. Then her father asked, "What about them?"

"Well, we can't just leave them out there for the horse killers!"

"There isn't anything else we can do," Pace said.

"Couldn't we drive them . . . corral them here?"

"Corral them here!" Her father nearly exploded. "We're going to pay hell to feed our own stock through the summer if the rains don't come."

Sandra flinched. She had known what his answer would be. Still, she couldn't give up. "Maybe we could break them, then sell them for riding horses at Three Bends."

Pace Bradford laughed. "You're lucky if there are three sound horses in that whole mangy, spavined lot," he snorted.

Sandra knew he was right. They might be tough and they might be beautiful. Yet they were outlaw horses, wild animals, and there weren't many among them likely to make pleasure-riding mounts.

Bone-tired, frustrated, Sandra felt close to tears again. Once again, she knew another band of wild horses would be driven by plane and jeeps until they staggered into Three Bends a glassy-eyed ghost troop, blood from tortured lungs crusting their raw nostrils, and she felt her vitality sag, felt the last tendon of endurance shredded.

Mrs. Webley was aware of the girl's condition if the men were not. "Can't we talk about this tomorrow?" she asked.

Pace Bradford got the message. "Let's all get some sleep," he said, getting up and stretching.

Sandra felt a sudden chill, though the room was hot, and she pulled the light bathrobe closer around her. "Tomorrow!" she said. "Tomorrow will be too late!"

Pace Bradford threw out his arms in a gesture of exasperation. Even the sympathetic expressions on the faces of the ranch hands hardened. As if to end the controversy, the father turned his back. "There's nothing can be done," he said in a cold, calculating tone. "Say the word and we'll all ride out tomorrow to get your stallion. What's more, I'll not have him gelded if that's what you want. What happens to the rest of the herd just can't be our concern. You must understand that."

So saying, Pace Bradford walked to the open staircase and went upstairs. When they heard his bedroom door close, the four ranch hands got up. Chase Long gave the girl a half smile, an almost apologetic look. Then the four trooped out, and with Mrs. Webley's arm around her shoulders, Sandra mounted the stairs to her room.

The moon had come around so that it laid a white path across her beige rug. Without turning down the spread, she lay on top of the bed still in her robe. Tired as she was, sleep seemed like a fleeting shadow — something which would not settle to comfort her.

In the end, she fell into a restless sleep, dreaming of wild horses galloping. Like reruns of the same film, the horses galloped by, then galloped again. She knew she was dreaming and she tried to awaken, but the magic key to wakefulness would not come to open her mind so she might sit up and build some fanciful, childish picture of the plane cracking up, of the jeeps turning over . . . and the horses running triumphantly away, free forever.

Sweat covered her forehead, and even as she slept, her legs, her arms, her lungs . . . seemed leaden. Then, as if suddenly stung by an invisible jet of electric clarity, she sat bolt upright in bed. It was incomprehensible, but from some inner sanctum over which she had no control, all the answers to the multiple questions had suddenly been answered. She now knew exactly what she must do, and precisely how she must go about doing it.

She got up quietly, and as quietly put on her dusty blue jeans, the sweat-stained shirt. Carrying her riding boots, she crept down the stairs, held her breath when the screen door creaked, and then tiptoed out onto the porch. She carried her boots all the way to the corral before putting them on.

Then when a horse nickered, when one of the hounds bayed, she held her breath and watched the house for lights.

Amazingly, she was no longer tired. The adrenaline flowed. Her heart thumped forcefully and faithfully to give strength to her purpose. From the tack room came her saddle, a canteen, a rope . . .

Then walking past Step-And-A-Half, who slept soundly on three legs, she threw the saddle blanket on a fresh mount, a little cutting horse, a bay they called Brandy.

She led the horse from the corral, led her across the hard-packed yard, led her through a gate, and then at the edge of the prairie she mounted up.

Quiet as a ghost rider on a ghost horse, she followed a fence line. The hound bayed again. A coyote answered. Sandra glanced back. A light came on in the bathroom of the ranch house. Then it went out. She rode on with only the stars and the night creatures of soft feathers and soft furs to know about her passing.

9

Brandy, the little bay cutting horse, picked her way in the dark carefully among all such pitfalls as prairie-dog holes, sliding shale on the occasional barren hillocks, low bushes with reaching, thorny fingers, in some of the draws . . . until, just as the stars began to pale, she came to the fringe of cottonwoods into which Sandra had driven Rimrock Red and the band of wild horses.

The horses had drifted back out from beneath the sheltering trees, and now, as she rested her horse, she could dimly see them grazing in a loosely held knot of animals with Rimrock, like a satellite horse, still revolving — at a safe distance from the white stallion — around the perimeter of the herd.

It would not do, nor was it necessary, to disturb them now. So she got down, loosed the saddle cinch to give Brandy breathing room and permitted the little bay mare to graze.

Smoothing a place for herself beneath a small cottonwood, she sat to watch the stars wink out until at last there was only the defiant morning star, Venus, shining almost brazenly in the east until at last the rays from a still hidden sun finally extinguished it.

The hot sun put a yellow tinge to a sea of prairie grasses. The loose knot of horses on the prairie began to bunch up as the hammerheaded, spotted mare prepared to lead them to water. "So now," Sandra told herself, "is the time."

She cinched up the saddle and swung aboard. Slowly she circled the band of horses and staying far enough away to keep them from breaking into a run got them drifting once again back toward the trees.

Brandy knew her job. Without ever breaking out of a slow trot, she turned in strays and kept the whole band pointed in the direction her rider had delicately indicated she wanted them to travel.

Only Rimrock proved recalcitrant. Still excited by the prospect of cutting out a harem for himself, he went off at wild tempting tangents, only to come back high-headed and indignant that one or another of the mares hadn't accepted his invitation to a tryst.

But Sandra did not worry about Rimrock. She knew that where the mares went, he would follow, and it was her purpose to have the little band drift with as little commotion as possible to a place of temporary safety.

Beneath the trees the herd began to string out, and Brandy had her work cut out for her, as the younger animals went off on exploratory side trips to taste some tempting herbage or simply kick up their heels at a fleeing cottontail.

Several times Sandra had to hold Brandy back to permit the horses to regroup of their own volition. Gradually, the strays and stragglers pulled to within the lead mare's influence, and once more Sandra would move Brandy with such subtlety the horses never realized they were being maneuvered into the forest, higher up into the foothills.

The last several hundred yards of the forest drive were the easiest. The horses, smelling water, quickened their pace and moved in a brisk line directly to the little box canyon which Sandra knew held a sparkling spring pool and a green park of luscious grasses buttressed by almost sheer canyon walls.

Sandra held the bay back, permitted the band to "find" the pool and the park themselves. Then when the horses had drunk their fill, and were scattered again to graze, she watered the mare she was riding. Now that the white stallion had eased off out onto grassland, Rimrock moved within easy roping distance to drink.

Sandra made no move to try to rope him. Instead, she talked to him gently, as she had so often, and he stood, muzzle dripping silver strands of water, looking at her intently with ears at strict attention to her dulcet tones:

"Maybe later, fellow. Maybe later. Maybe

when this is all over we'll ride again. There's time. Lots of time. All summer. A whole lifetime."

Brandy watered, Sandra turned her away from the herd and walked her back through the trees over the trail they had just traversed. Long before she came to the prairie edge, she heard the plane. Now she could listen to its drone with equanimity. The pilot would not find the horses. Even if he did, he'd not be able to do anything except perhaps scatter the animals out among the trees.

Sandra dismounted at the prairie edge to watch the plane as it made wide sweeps, looking for the herd. Tired as she was she had to smile. The initial segment of her plan had been successfully completed.

She remained alert to the situation, however, but kept herself concealed. Staying to the trees, she watched until the plane at last disappeared over the searing white horizon in the direction of Three Bends.

Now, even at a walk, sweat darkened the little horse's withers and chest. Sandra got down sometimes and walked. Even if she might ride her mount hard and ruthlessly if such were required, she would never exert an animal if there was no necessity.

She was not too surprised to see her father in the distance. As she fully expected, he had ridden out to search for her. He was coming from afar, another rider with him, and she knew by the way they were pushing their animals that she had been sighted.

No matter what he said, her mind was made

up. She was eighteen. She was her own woman. If she would never carelessly disregard any of his demands, or even his wishes, in this thing she was determined. He would have to know that she was resolved, that the odds no longer mattered. That come high water or any kind of burning desert hell, she would see the thing through — put the herd out of reach of the horse killers.

As soon as the two approaching horsemen were close enough to see she was riding high and well in the saddle, they slowed their horses to a walk. Chase Long was the man who had come to help hunt her.

Finally the two men halted their sweating and lathered mounts and permitted her to ride up to them. As the distance between them diminished, Sandra braced herself for a tongue-lashing. Instead her father almost laconically said, "Good morning. Rather warm for riding, wouldn't you say?"

Sandra couldn't help but laugh. It was a laugh as much of relief as amusement at her father's almost droll greeting. But she was in no mood to be dissuaded, to be put off by his bit of play-acting. So she said, "Hot? Yes. But not as hot as it's likely to get before long."

"And what's that supposed to mean?"

"Just this, Dad. I'm taking that herd of horses out of here."

"And just where to you plan to take them?"

"To the Rantan Reservation."

The look on both men's faces was first one of disbelief, then amusement. They were sure she was joking.

"It's the nearest public land with range for horses, the only place where they'll be safe," Sandra said. "I'm not kidding. I'm going to move that herd to the Rantan Reservation."

A bridle jingled as the little bay horse slapped her head down at a fly. Now that Sandra had put her plan into words, she could hardly believe it herself.

"I've got all summer. I can't think of a better way to spend it."

Her father spoke slowly, as if weighing each word. "You mean," he asked, "you would do something like that just for the adventure?"

Sandra lowered her eyes. "No," she said quietly. "I'm doing it because I just can't stand by and see those horses prodded across the prairie the way those men drove in the first herd."

"Do you know what such a venture entails?" her father asked.

"Not really, I suppose."

"Well, at least you're not cocky," Pace Bradford said. "Now let's see," he went on. "There are nearly fifty miles of desert to cross, a mountain range, and the only pass through the range is a four-lane superhighway buzzing with traffic. Then, even if you got across the desert and over the mountain" — his words were cracking now like pistol shots — "you would run into a valley of vineyards, and you can be sure that the grape growers, gentle people though they be, would be forced to meet your band of wild horses with shotguns, no less. And if you managed to get a half-dozen head past the grape growers . . ."

Sandra's eyes flashed to the face of Chase

53

Long, where she found only bewilderment. Her own hopes at completing such a trek seemed to gutter in the long list of seemingly insurmountable obstacles listed by her father. "Where are the horses now?" he asked.

"I've herded them into a little box canyon."

"What makes you think they'll stay there?"

"They'll stay. For a couple of days anyway. There's water. There's good grazing. They won't come down until the grass is short."

Pace turned his horse. Long fell in alongside him. Sandra, on the little bay, trailed. Except for the creak of leather, the jingle of bridles and the muffled thud of hooves, the hot, still air lifted no other sounds. But then clearly, and defiantly, Sandra said, "Well, you'll see! I'm going to do it!"

10

That there would be a confrontation Sandra
never doubted. That her father knew it too was
obvious because he avoided her throughout the
day, hoping perhaps that in time she might
change her mind.

Supper that night was a mostly silent time,
but then it came while she was standing in front
of the gun rack trying to decide whether she
should take a rifle along, and if so, which one.

The ranch hands had gone back to the bunkhouse, and Mrs. Webley could be heard in the
kitchen. Pace Bradford was still sitting at the
table. Suddenly throwing his napkin down, he
came at her straight and hard as a diving hawk.

"You know I'm not going to let you do it!" he said.

"And how do you propose to stop me?" she asked, her voice subdued, her emotions in control.

For Pace Bradford, a man who usually got his way merely by crooking a forefinger, it was a deft thrust. He might have dealt with her anger, but to have her sharply as a knife cut quietly right to the heart of the matter put him off balance. And it showed in the red which glowed through his richly browned cheeks.

"But, honey," he said, swallowing now to keep control, "it can't be done! You've no idea of what it means to herd a band of wild horses across a desert, over mountains . . ." He hesitated, almost expectantly, as if she suddenly might relent, reconsider, end it all right there without further argument.

"Dad, let's sit down," Sandra said. She moved to the table, but Pace remained on his feet. Facing him, she said, "I've got something I want to ask you. I want you to think about it before you answer me." She hesitated, then added, "Please?"

If before Pace had been only dimly aware that the child he'd raised was no ordinary child, but a person cast into his own mold, he knew it for certain now. It was in her eyes, her demeanor. He took a chair, sat down heavily, and prepared to permit her to deal with him on even terms.

Moving closer, so she was standing almost over him, Sandra said, "I want to ask you a question, and I want you to think about it, and I want you to answer honestly."

Bradford narrowed his eyes a trifle, but she looked at him squarely and asked, "If I were a boy . . . if I were your son, and if I was determined to do this thing, would you stop me?"

Pace's eyes widened. Before he could say anything, Sandra put up a hand. "Now think about it first. If I were your son instead of your daughter, a boy you'd raised to know his own mind, to be self-reliant, the way you did me, would you stand in my way?"

Pace started to answer. "Hear me out, Dad," she said. "Listen to what I've got to say." Sandra continued quietly: "You taught me to ride. You taught me to rope. You taught me to fish, to shoot, to brand a calf, to break a horse. You taught me all the things I need to know."

The moment brought back many memories. She had to pause, to catch herself, because she could feel tears pooling, and she knew that tears would be disastrous.

She got hold of herself. Even stronger this time, she continued: "What I'm saying, Dad, is that you've made me capable, that you have made me as durable as any son you might have had."

She took a deep breath. "Now let's suppose," she said, "that I was the son. And suppose this son wanted to do this thing. And you would tell him, of course, what a damn fool he was. And you would argue with him that it couldn't be done. And you would say he was crazy. But then, and this is the important thing — the crux of the whole matter — in the end, if he insisted, you would be proud. And maybe after that son rode away to get on with what he had to do, you might even brag to the hands about him, about how there goes 'a chip off the old block.'

"Well, Dad," she continued, her voice rising slightly and taking on a fresh note of insistence, "I too am a chip off the old block. Just because an accident of conception made me female makes me no less a person, no less capable than if it were the other way around. And sometimes maybe you forget that. Sometimes, maybe you still wish I were a boy . . ."

Pace Bradford started to protest. Sandra beat him to it by saying, "It doesn't really make any difference. It really isn't important anymore."

Pace Bradford was looking at the floor now. She wanted to go over and put an arm around him, but she refrained. Instead, she said, "Don't you see, Dad, if I were your son you'd be proud that I wanted to do this damn fool thing because you'd be proud I had enough guts to try it. What's more, you'd be proud I cared enough to want to save the wild horses. So why can't you honor Sandra Bradford, your daughter, with as much consideration?"

At that moment, Mrs. Webley, who must have overheard, decided to play her role, a part she had become so deft at. It was nice timing, because father and daughter had come to an embarrassing impasse.

Pace Bradford would need time to assimilate, to think over the things Sandra had said. Sandra would need time to steel herself to proceed, to do the thing.

Mrs. Webley's interruption came in the form of an innocuous question, "Coffee, anyone?" Both Sandra and Pace accepted gratefully.

11

Next morning before she rode off, Pace Bradford advised her to take a .30-30-caliber carbine instead of her little .22-caliber rifle. "You might have accidents. You might have to shoot an injured horse. The twenty-two isn't gun enough."

The announcement that she might have to shoot a horse shook Sandra. Her hands trembled a little as she picked up the gun.

Pace had been up with her since before dawn. He helped her with her bedroll, took down an oversized canteen from a rack, picked out such dehydrated food as the hands took on the trail and sealed them in plastic, and suggested she carry ten pounds of oats for her horse.

"She'll be working like she never worked

before, even though you are fifty pounds lighter than the average ranch hands who have been riding her. Those horses won't want to cross the desert. She'll hold up better if you grain her," Pace had advised.

They had decided that Brandy would be the better horse. "She's tougher, more wiry than Step-And-A-Half. What's more, she's older, wiser, less likely to spook," Pace had said.

They had looked at a map Pace had drawn for her, and decided that she might be able to leave the horses along the way for a fast trip into Sago for supplies.

Pace said the desert trek should be started in the morning. "Then by night you'll be halfway, and then the last half will be in the cool of the night and likely you'll have less trouble."

He had told her he didn't think she could sleep on the desert trek because "They'll turn back if you do."

Toughest part, they both agreed, would be getting the horses over the mountains and then around the vineyards in the valley on the other side.

"Maybe take the road just before dawn. Probably won't be much, if any, traffic. There is no other pass through the mountains. I guess you've got maybe eight miles of road. The herd will have to be well grazed when you try the road so you can hustle them right on through."

Sandra had asked him about the vineyards. "I just don't know," he said. "Probably you'll have to find a way around them. The grape growers, mostly of Spanish and Italian ancestry, are good people. But they value their vines, most of which have been imported. Even so, if they are aware of what you are trying to do, I'm sure they'd help, because that is the nature of these people. But mostly, when you hit the vineyards you'll have to play it by ear. Maybe that's the way it's going to be anyway, all along the trail."

Father and daughter were very close that morning in the home before the dawn. Closer than they'd been since Sandra's mother had died, since the day Mrs. Webley came and Sandra, a girl of ten, had cried because she had falsely assumed that her father was replacing his dead wife, her mother, with another woman.

There in the musty storeroom which attached to the back of the house, with its smell of dry coffee, onions, dill, and mothballs between the walls to discourage the mice, ants, and other insects, Pace put a hand on his daughter's shoulder and said, "I'm afraid for you, Sandy."

Sandy! He hadn't called her that in years, not since her tawny hair had darkened, not since she had been a curious six-year-old wandering recklessly between the legs of horses to snap flies off their rounding bellies.

Sandra tried to keep the conversation on the light side. Not because she didn't feel deeply her father's concern for her, but because she couldn't afford to risk losing her advantage, weakening her resolve. Several times she was close to the warm relief tears might have afforded. But to succumb to them, to throw herself into her father's arms might have eroded what strengths she needed to ride off. Once on her way she knew it would be easier. Then, even if she wanted to, there would be no turning back.

So in answer to her father's fears, she turned a deliberate smile and, with a voice which belied her own concern, said, "After all, Dad, I'm not going to the North Pole!"

It was a relief for her when they left the intimacy of the kitchen and came into the living room, where the gear was piled.

"Think I've got everything?" she asked.

Pace went over the list again, checking off items he had written on a piece of brown wrapping paper. "Matches," he said. "My God, I almost forgot the matches!"

"Lucky it's only matches," the girl said. "Much more stuff and I'd have to trail a pack-horse along."

"It looks like a lot," Pace said, "but there isn't really much weight. Still I think we'd be better off to use a couple bran sacks instead of saddle-bags. Saddlebags can pound pretty hard on a horse's kidneys, especially if you have to do a lot of hard riding. Sacks will ride better. Fill each half full and we can tie them down."

They moved the gear out onto the porch where it could be packed and transferred to Brandy's back. The hands were coming up from the bunkhouse now, and behind them a silver dollar of a sun perched precariously on the horizon almost as if wondering whether it was worth the sweaty effort of once more crossing the sky.

Breakfast was uncommonly quiet. Instead of coming up with suggestions, offering advice, the hands busied themselves with their food. Perhaps Chase Long summed up their feelings best when he said, "You'll have to take it as it comes."

Only Mrs. Webley tried for the light touch. "It'll be just like a vacation," she said, unconvincingly. "I slept out under the stars once. That's something!" But this time even she couldn't ease the tension. Finally even she succumbed to the knife-sharp silence and breakfast was finished in quick fork stabs.

The gun went into the scabbard with a hard, leathery "thunk" of finality.

Sandra turned to look at the four ranch hands, then at Mrs. Webley, who seemed on the verge of tears. For an instant, she almost succumbed to the desire to throw herself into her father's arms, to reassure him of her love.

But the moment passed. Pace Bradford stepped forward. He put a hand on her shoulder. His face was taut and his eyebrows almost met. Then, as if he felt he had to try just one last time, he said, "Maybe if someone went along . . ."

"Dad!" the girl interrupted.

"No, I guess not."

Awkwardly he held out a hand. She was just as awkward in taking it. Fingers clasped and fell apart, and then Sandra was in the saddle.

With a whoop to cover the embarrassment they both must have felt, Sandra kicked the little cutting horse into a fast gallop. She circled the five men and the woman, half-turning in the saddle to see how her bedroll, how the half-filled bran sacks were riding.

Satisfied that everything was in place and

secure, she pulled Brandy back to a walk, and facing her away from the ranch buildings, she rode off, and she did not look back until she was a diminishing figure in the heat waves which were already making the prairie dance. Then she turned, put up a hand, and when she saw six hands come up to return the salute, she smiled faintly and then, setting her lips tightly, she looked west.

Part Two

12

Long before she could hear it, Sandra saw the plane. It was nearly noon, and she figured she had come fifteen miles. The plane was so distant when she first spotted it, it looked like a bluebottle fly hanging to the pale gauze of the horizon sky. Then it quickly increased from fly to eagle size, and shortly was discernible as an airplane.

Now its steady drone, as of a thousand bees, rasped at her nerves, and lest she give the pilot a clue to her direction, she swung Brandy about and started back in the direction of the ranch.

The pilot must have spotted her in the same moment that she turned the horse. Flying over for a closer look, he dived almost at once, and as the plane swept by, bending the prairie grasses with prop wash, she got a glimpse of a bearded pilot, his teeth bared in a wide grin.

Brandy skittered and Sandra had to rein her in lest she go flat out in panicky flight. She talked to the horse, reached over to pat her sleek neck, and by the time the plane had turned and made ready for a second pass, Sandra had the horse in hand.

Then the pilot turned on the siren, and like a wailing banshee the plane came hurtling. When Sandra ducked involuntarily as if to escape being decapitated by the swift, cutting passage of the undercarriage, she momentarily lost her seat and Brandy, sensing her loss of control, made a series of jackrabbit hops to send her flying through the air.

When she looked up, Brandy was headed for home and the pilot was wing-waggling triumphantly. Sandra hurled a few choice curse words borrowed from her treasure of ranch hand lingo, and then getting to her feet, brushed the dirt off her face, out of her hair, and began walking to where Brandy had finally stopped and was now grazing peacefully.

By the time she caught up with the horse, the plane had disappeared. Brandy was no further trouble, and back in the saddle she once again headed toward where the cottonwoods marked the entry point to the uplands, to where the box canyon was harboring the herd.

The plane would be back. If not today, then tomorrow. She couldn't believe they would give up that easily.

She put Brandy into a ground-consuming trot

and felt a sense of relief and of satisfaction when she could finally put the horse beneath the sheltering trees.

Within a half hour she could see the break in the trees. Urging Brandy into a fast trot, she came to the clearing and saw the band scattered widely across the grassy parkland. Rimrock Red was as far as he could get from the white stallion. Then as she rode closer to him she saw there was a curving wound arching down from his withers almost to his brisket.

So they had fought. Sandra supposed that was inevitable. She rode closer for a better look at the white stallion. There wasn't a mark on him.

Circling the herd so as not to disturb them, she got to the head of the canyon and, finding an elevated rocky bench from which she could look down, loosed Brandy's cinch and let her graze while she took a closer look at the equine family she had decided to mother and move.

She counted them. Not counting Rimrock, there were thirty-one. There were five foals — two colts and three fillies. Mostly the band was made up of blacks and bays, but there were three paints, a strawberry roan, a patchy white-gray "watch" horse with spooky white eyes, a couple of sorrels, and two grays.

There were at least four young stallions — perhaps yearlings not yet ready to challenge the white stallion. Otherwise their ages seemed to run the gamut, and she guessed the hammer-headed paint mare, a large gangling horse which gave the impression of being all joints, was not only the leader, but the oldest of the bunch.

As horseflesh she had to admit they were not a blue-ribbon lot. Her father would have called them "a gang of inbred, Roman-nosed, spavined cayuses." Yet a more careful look by a more discerning eye might have noticed Arabian, quarter horse, and characteristics of other familiar breeds — likely inherited from escaped ranch stock.

The white stallion was an especially fine specimen. He looked almost like a thoroughbred, but was generally much heavier, she thought, than any of the thoroughbreds she had ever seen.

Could be, she thought, he was a recent escapee from one ranch or another. There was no doubt he would improve the herd.

Having catalogued the herd, she made up her mind to let them graze here for at least this day. The horse hunters would never think to search among the high pines. Getting down from her perch on the ledge, she caught up Brandy, led her to a small grove of clustering pines and relieved her of the saddle, the packs, and then taking off her bridle, slipped a rope halter on the horse. Then she turned her loose.

Taking the big canteen, she walked carefully, so as not to spook the horses, down to the pool which was fed by bubbling springs. She poured the water from the canteen, filled it at the spring with fresh, cool, clear water, and then took a long drink.

Among the pines, then, she spread her bedroll, and gathered a few rocks to contain a fire. A small pile of dead branches, gathered quickly, was stacked beside the stones. Bran sacks of provisions and Brandy's oats were hung from a limb.

Then she sat on her bedroll and taking the ribbon out of her ponytail, shook her hair free. Carefully and tightly she wove her hair into two braids. She ripped the white hair ribbon into two lengths to tie the braid ends to keep them from unraveling. Then she lay back, rested on an elbow.

There was still plenty of grass in the clearing. What's more, the grass was of infinitely better quality than the horses were accustomed to. The sun quickly toughened prairie grasses, but even at this slight altitude, and surrounded by trees, the grass grew more slowly and retained its freshness longer.

The herd had several days of grass remaining should she decide not to move them right away. And who would ever think to look here, on the side of a mountain, for prairie horses? But the heat below would become increasingly fierce with every passing day, and she could not countenance undue delay, despite the fact that here in this lush place were few dangers for the horses, and it was an almost idyllic place to idle away — well, a whole summer!

After a while Sandra walked among the trees. The cushion of pine needles was like a velvet carpet. She took off her riding boots and carried them. A bright eye on the low limb of a pine brought her to an abrupt halt. It was a fool hen, native grouse. Aside from making an especially tasty meal, it would help stretch her food supply and so she began to stalk it.

But her caution was wasted on the bird because it exhibited no fear, only cocked its head from side to side. When the girl was within a couple of arm lengths of the grouse, she let fly with a boot. The bird came tumbling down, flopping and fluttering. Then before it could recover, Sandra was on it, and with a quick snap of her wrist, broke its neck.

As with even the most hardened of hunters, she stifled the tightening of sadness in her throat as she fingered and admired the many shades of earthy colors which made each feather a thing of separate beauty. Finding a log, she sat down and began to pluck the bird.

That night she let the fire burn down to a bed of red coals before she spitted the grouse on a green stick for broiling. When its skin had turned brown, crinkly and crisp, she put it on a rock, cut off a thigh, and ate hungrily.

The sun was long gone before she finished the grouse, but it was still light enough to see. So with a handful of dried dates to nibble on, she climbed to the rock bench to make a head count of the herd.

They were all there, some lying down, others sleeping on three legs, and some grazing. Rimrock Red was at a far end, almost under the trees, and watching the white stallion almost as though he were studying him.

Then if it was still stifling hot down on the prairie, here there was a little breeze, and under the trees it was cool. She went back to lie atop her bedroll and looked up. The stars were so low it seemed they were almost hanging like ornaments in the tops of the tallest trees — giant firs and pines — virgin timber. It was a silent world broken only by a snuffling horse or the sound of an unshod hoof against a rock.

Lying there she had no qualms about the task, the trek ahead. She would simply drive the horses to the Rantan Reservation, put a rope on Rimrock, and then take him home. It seemed that easy in this quiet, cool — this peaceful place.

13

She stayed an extra day in the box canyon because the horses were reluctant to leave such a wealth of tender grass with its little gold mine of water.

It was an idyllic sabbatical. There in the green amphitheater between the rising stone cliffs she lived in a separate world of unutterable peace and quiet. In all her life she had never felt so keenly alive. Nothing was unimportant. Even a drop of dew, shivering with reflections on a pine needle, could keep her entranced until it dropped like a tear.

And the nights: sky soft black velvet sparkling with sequins, forest aromatic with pine resin, sliding shadow of an owl, distant lonely heartache of a wailing coyote, barely audible music of spring water on little stones, fire glow diminishing in darkening coals, grass cool under hand, breeze a kiss on her cheeks . . .

Twice during those two days she thought she heard the far-off drone of the plane, and it was an almost sweet sort of revenge to think about the pilot's bewilderment as he looked for a horse herd which had quite mysteriously disappeared.

They would never think to look in the foot-hills, of that she was quite sure. A rancher might, but these men were neither cowmen nor horsemen, but likely — according to a consensus of her father's ranch hands — "just some of Three Bends' street-corner opportunists looking to make a quick buck in borrowed jeeps and a rented plane."

When she got ready to move the horses on the morning of the third day, they were reluctant to desert such fine pasturage. It took some hard riding and persistent prodding to get them filing out among the trees, down the slopes, back to the prairie.

It was near the middle of the morning when they finally came to the prairie and were wading once more through undulating grass. She pulled up then, and with the map her father had prepared plotted a course across the prairie.

With the stub of a pencil she carried in a shirt pocket, she drew a faint line westerly, and then wrote at the top on the ample white margin surrounding the map:

"Third morning out. June 30. Hot. Horses complacent. Here we go!"

Well-fed, the horses, after a flurry of head tossing, whinnying, and a general milling reluctance to file west, finally gave in to Brandy's swift and darting competence. Then Sandra fell back, never moving in on the herd so long as their general direction was westerly, and so long as one or another didn't stray to graze.

So the morning went well, and Sandra was about to congratulate herself, when the plane came back. When she first heard it the horses were strung out in a ragged almost single-file line with the lead mare up front, the white stallion bringing up the rear, and Rimrock, as usual, spending his precious energy orbiting nervously as a buzzing fly around the long line of march.

On sighting the plane, Sandra stopped Brandy, pulled down the broad brim of her hat against the glare of the sun to wait and to watch. Like a hunting hawk the plane was nosing down to start its stoop, and now there were no trees toward which to flee. Now there was nothing but open prairie, and who could hide in knee-high grass?

The horses had heard the plane. Already they had broken into a trot as if remembering past assaults from the sky by the big bird that screamed. All ears were laid back, all nostrils flared, all breathing quickened as if the herd intuitively knew about the death march which ended in bloodied mouths.

The plane took its time. The pilot could afford to let the tension mount, and frighten them out of their wits.

But Sandra was not without a plan. She had known the plane would be back.

Whipping off her hat, she kneed Brandy into a convulsive gallop. Waving her hat wildly, she went charging among the horses and the line of march, compressing the band until it was all bunched up. Wheeling the little cutting horse into an abrupt about-face, she went charging back whooping and waving her hat. When she hit the milling band the horses exploded like seeds from a pod in every direction.

Once more she careened Brandy into a tight turn and came racing back. This time the plane, siren screaming, was there unwittingly to help her further scatter the horses until they were fleeing far and wide in all directions like leaves ahead of a whirling wind.

At once she pulled Brandy to a jarring halt. She glanced up at the plane. Let him round them up. Now let him try to gather the widely separated herd into a knot of horses cohesive enough for a coordinated drive back to the loading pens at Three Bends.

She knew no airplane could do it. She knew even she and Brandy couldn't do it. She knew that unless the pilot could perch on a cloud somewhere and wait until the horses regrouped of their own volition, he had once more been defeated. It would take more gas than the little plane carried to wander in waiting circles for the mustangs to come back together.

The pilot must have known it too. Immediately he concentrated on once again panicking Brandy and unseating Sandra. Once more she got a glimpse of the grin in the bushy face as the plane swept by.

Brandy trembled, took a few short hops under tightened rein, but she did not bolt. Sandra jammed her hat on, grabbed the horse with heels, knees, and thighs. The plane came diving back. The blast of air washed the horse's mane back into Sandra's face.

Head down, hands double-wound around the reins, Sandra awaited the next assault. It came with a seemingly reckless abandon. The pilot put the plane so low the undercarriage mowed down prairie grass and the wing of the craft came slicing past within ten feet of Sandra and the horse.

Brandy jumped sideways. The surprise move nearly unseated Sandra. Then the little horse, still under tight reins, pivoted in several swift circles. Sandra grabbed for leather. The horse reared, but she hung on. Then Brandy stood trembling.

At once Sandra leaped out of the saddle. With a quick jerk she slid the .30-30-caliber carbine from the scabbard. Then dropping the reins, she waved the horse away and waited.

Already the plane was turning. Its nose came down, its speed increased, its propeller was a silvery wash of sunlight aimed straight at her.

Sandra braced her feet. Once more she yanked at the wide brim of her hat to bring it low over her forehead. She held the carbine with both hands halfway to her shoulder.

In all the world there was nothing except the strident siren and the roaring engine. The noise suffocated senses. The plane was coming in another senseless charge, and every atom of her being begged that she throw herself flat, hug the earth, get down and out of the way.

But if fear can be a sometimes debilitating emotion, there's no better cure for it than anger and hatred. And Sandra was mad. She hated this airplane, this man, with all the deep down hatred she had for men who would drive a horse until the blood from his lungs is crusted black on his nostrils.

Still for all of it, she was coldly, almost fascinatingly alert. She knew what she meant to do, and she knew how she meant to do it. If he did not get the message, then the onus would be on him. If he came again, it would be with the sure knowledge of what to expect.

The plane was there and the gun was up. Looking down the barrel she saw the face, and in the split instant of passing, saw the white teeth fade behind the bristles of face hair.

Like a lightning streak it was so imprinted on the back of her eyes in that place where the brain takes over, that the image of the grin fading kept flashing back again and again to her even after the plane had made a lazy circle and was heading for Three Bends.

Lowering the gun, Sandra sank limply to the ground. With her head just above the prairie grass she looked around. The horses were scattered almost as far as she could see, but already there was a general movement as they gravitated back toward their guiding star, the old hammer-headed mare.

Brandy hadn't run too far, and was already grazing. Tonight, for sure, she'd have to grain the little horse. Tonight also, she'd slip some cartridges into the rifle's magazine. Then with a flip of the wrist she would be able to lever a cartridge into the chamber and be ready to shoot.

14

It took the horses nearly two hours to reassemble, and then the march was resumed. Several times during the afternoon Sandra consulted the map, though there were no landmarks to orient on, nothing but flat prairie and the vague horizon, which seemed to come near and then retreat, grow bright and then grow dim in the wavering heat waves.

The line she had drawn on the map in the morning was little more than an educated guess ending where her father had marked an X locating a waterhole at which she meant to spend the night.

She had been depending on that waterhole, and she reasoned that the horses knew about it too and, unless she was too far off course, would automatically gravitate to it.

She was right. Just as night absconded with the last rays of evening, the horses began running and she knew her objective was not far off. Sandra held Brandy back until the anxious neighing of the herd told her something was amiss. She kneed her horse into a quick canter to close with the herd, which was milling in confusion. She rode through them, scattering horses, and came to the waterhole.

It was dry.

For a while she sat and even the light of the stars was enough to see that where the white alkaline wash marked the bottom of the hole there was not a single drop of water.

While she sat looking, the lead mare edged toward the hole and went sliding down the sides. Then she began to paw. Sandra slipped from the saddle, and when she walked into the hole the hammerheaded mare jumped out. Dropping to her knees, Sandra dug in the sand with her hands.

Nothing.

The air seemed to drain from her lungs and with it, so too her hopes. Without a long, last drink she would not dare take the horses out into the desert. Back on Brandy she wondered what to do. The desert was only a few miles ahead. Already the prairie grasses had thinned and there was mesquite and the occasional cactus. Go back? Back where and to what?

She rode a little way from the dry waterhole, got down. Gathering some mesquite pods and branches, and a few dry cow chips, she built a small fire, and with water from her canteen in a small all-purpose pan dissolved some dehydrated beef and dehydrated potatoes.

The stars brightened considerably even as she ate, and while wrestling with the problem of how to proceed, the wild horses, still snuffling around the dry waterhole, suddenly sounded an alarm with strident whinnies.

Sandra jumped to her feet, stood for several seconds, and then with almost animal instinctiveness backed quickly out of the glow of the fire and with feet braced and hands held ready as though to ward off an attack, she waited.

Rattler? Maybe, she thought. Puma? Bear? Never. Not this far from their mountain refuge. Coyote? Could be. Maybe looking for a drink too. But if that's all it was, a mangy, flea-bitten, no-account coyote . . .

She bent forward in a listening attitude, but the horses were making too much noise, and then suddenly, right on the edge of the firelight she had just left — like a gnome out of nowhere — there appeared a small man with cheeks ruddy as ripe apples above the snowfall of a flowing beard. And, looking over his shoulder, big eyes blinking in the light of the flames, was a long-eared, seriocomic burro.

"Your horses?" the man asked gently, a small smile marking the spot where his mouth had been hiding in the thick beard.

Sandra didn't know whether to collapse to her knees and weep with relief, or strike out at him sharply, asking, "You might have given me some warning, announced that you were coming!"

Actually, she only nodded in the affirmative to his question, and then in a small voice, "Yes, in a way. In a way they are my horses."

"Mind if I sit at your fire?" the man asked.

"Well . . . no . . . if you'd like . . . of course. Please do."

The man dropped the rope with which he had been leading the burro, stepped forward and then asked, "Join me?"

At that she suddenly, and for no good reason, felt like laughing. Instead she walked into the circle of light, and then they both sat separated by the tiny flames.

"Eat?" she asked, gesturing toward the nearly empty pan.

"No, thanks. I already have."

"Waterhole dry." He did not make it a question, but said it as if he knew that, of course, it would be dry.

She only nodded.

"Going far?" the man asked.

"Well, actually yes." She was reluctant to tell him about her plan. He might try to talk her out of it, as the others had done.

"Across the desert?"

Sandra did not reply right away, but then said, "Yes, across the desert," and she added, "I hope."

"I know where there's water," the man said, in a noncommittal, offhand tone.

Sandra's head snapped up, and she was looking squarely into a pair of bemused, twinkling eyes beneath bushy white brows.

"Near here?" she asked.

"Not too far."

"But how come the horses don't go to it?"

"It's a tiny basin, a little way out on the desert. They'd have had no occasion to visit it. They wouldn't know where it's at."

The sudden relief Sandra felt left her momentarily speechless. Finally she asked, "Could you direct me to it?"

"Better yet, I'll take you there."

"Oh, you wouldn't have to."

"Be my pleasure."

They were both quiet then. From the direction of the dry waterhole, where the horses waited as if the water might magically reappear, there was the sound of much snuffling and blowing, the sound of unshod hooves on the dry earth, and the occasional piercingly sharp whinny of a thirsty animal.

Finally the man asked, "Have you ever crossed the desert?"

Sandra shook her head.

"Isn't it rather risky?"

"Perhaps. But I have to do it."

"Mind telling me why?"

Sandra stared intently at her fingernails, broken and dirty now. When she didn't say anything, the man asked, "Aren't those feral horses out there?"

The girl looked up. "Yes, they're wild."

"I thought so, but I'll bet my burro, Bessie, that you aren't a commercial horse killer."

"No, I'm not," Sandra said. "Actually" — she hesitated and then continued — "my name is

Sandra Bradford, and I'm trying to save them from the horse killers."

"I believe it," the man said, "but how?"

"I'm driving them to the Rantan Reservation," she began, and then in a quick, brief recital told him the whole story, about the airplane and even about Rimrock Red. When she had finished, she asked, "Do you think I'm crazy?"

The man appeared bemused. Then he said, "Yes, I think you are crazy — a little, anyway. But don't be alarmed. We're indebted to crazy people for some of our great music, great paintings — poetry."

"You're very kind," the girl said.

"Not really, because, you see, I'm a little crazy myself."

Sandra could believe that literally, else why would he be wandering the prairie with a burro? But proffering him a small smile, she asked politely, "What makes you crazy?"

"I'm a gold prospector."

"Oh?"

"Well, not really," the old man went on to explain. "I'm not really looking for a lode, but for three months of every year I go into the foothills to pan gold. It is my way of relaxing, getting away from it all."

"Ever find gold?"

"Oh, I always find gold. For years it was hardly enough to pay for the supplies I used. Then when the price of gold soared out of sight, I found I could pan enough dust to actually make some money."

"What do you do when you aren't panning gold?"

"Well, mostly I read and write and I think a lot." The old man chuckled, as if his answer amused him.

"Sounds like a nice life."

"The best. But now tell me, what prompted you to decide to herd these horses to safety, to drive them all the way to Rantan?"

Hesitantly Sandra told him of the cruelty of the horse killers.

The old man clucked sympathetically. "It goes on all the time."

"But why doesn't someone stop it?"

"People would if they could see what you saw. As it is, they only read about it. Then on the same page they read about millions starving in Africa. They read about children being bombed in Cambodia. They read about murder and rape in their own cities. So the horse doesn't have a chance."

"When you put it like that," Sandra said, "you make what I'm doing seem very unimportant, almost silly."

"Oh, no. Not at all." The old man put up his hands to his long, white beard. "Precisely the opposite. You are doing something good. In this instance it doesn't matter that you are saving horses instead of people, but it does matter that you care and are willing to make a sacrifice to do something."

Sandra started to interrupt, but the old man raised a hand and continued. "Look at it this way," he went on. "If everyone did the right thing, the good thing within their own little sphere of influence, if they worked at it . . ." He hesitated, and then quietly and undramatically said, "Then ultimately we would have a better world."

"But horses?" Sandra protested weakly.

"Horses or sparrows. Eskimos or Englishmen. It's as simple as that. All things inch us forward. It all counts."

It was a strange conversation out there in the darkness of the vast prairie by the little fire with a band of wild horses milling about a dry waterhole. A strange conversation between a young woman with a dirty face and a little old man with an immaculate snow-white beard.

Sandra looked thoughtful now. "But when I read history," she ventured, "it seems we as humans aren't making any advances, that we always fall back into the same old errors. That despite everything we make the same mistakes over and over. So where's the gain?"

"Of course, of course," the old man interrupted. "It seems that way. But take the long view — and that's the only legitimate view — and you must admit that man has come a long, long way as a compassionate human being since the days of the cave. He's even made some small advances since the time of Christ."

Now it was Sandra's turn to laugh. ". . . 'some small advances since the time of Christ' . . ." she quoted him. "When you compress time that way it makes sense."

"Of course it does. And remember this too, man is the only animal capable of true compassion. To quote William Blake, '. . . mercy has a human heart, pity a human face . . .'"

The moon had risen in the east and climbed high enough to put a pale, silvery glow on the grasses. In the little light the mass of horses gradually took shape, became individuals. The fire diminished, sparked once and then only glowed.

"Can you drive the horses at night?" the old man asked.

"I think so."

"Well, maybe we ought to travel then. If we start now, and everything goes right, we might make the waterhole by daybreak."

The horses were reluctant to move. A half-dozen times Sandra got them started, and then one or another would cut back and the entire herd would follow. Finally, however, they moved with the swift little cutting horse whipping left and right to keep the stragglers in line.

It was a strange, almost ghostly procession, with the old man and his burro bringing up the rear. Almost at once the prairie sod gave way to shifting sand, to knolls of shale, to reaching and thorny cacti.

Unseen by the man or the girl, horned toads watched unblinking. Little lizards scurried with a dry rustle. A tiny desert owl sailed over. On and on and on . . . and then when the first streak of light was a sharp sliver in the east, the horses smelled the water and broke into a wild gallop.

"I'll be leaving now," the old man said, after filling a canteen where the spring was a tiny trickle above the basin of the waterhole.

At once Sandra felt a chill of apprehension. It had been comforting for at least one night to shift responsibility to someone else's shoulders.

"Here." The old man handed her a note he had scribbled on a paper torn from a small notebook he had taken from a pocket. She took the note. Then he offered her his hand. She shook it. He took the lead line and the burro obediently followed him out across the sand.

When he was a diminishing figure among the cacti she looked down at the note:

"Good luck. And please write to tell me how you made out. Don't forget. It is important. Paul Pelham, Room 414, Pelham Hall, University of Branden."

Paul Pelham! She should have known! It should have occurred to her. Professor Pelham. Pulitzer Prize winner. Once nominated for the Nobel Prize. It had been in all the papers, the magazines, on television. Paul Pelham, the writer-philosopher who to refurbish his soul, went panning for gold each summer.

Would wonders never cease, Sandra Bradford thought, as she sat beside the trickling spring above where the horses still were jostling one another for a chance at the waterhole.

Professor Pelham out here in the desert with a burro named Bessie. Professor Pelham to give her assurance, to make her feel that what she was doing was not silly, but in fact, as he had put it, "something good . . ."

Sandra arose to face the blazing sun and the burning sands. She pulled the map from her hip pocket. On the white margin she wrote:

"Fourth morning out. July 1. Desert waterhole. You'd never guess who I met. Dammit, I'll make it."

15

The plane came back that morning. It circled well out of rifle range, then turning tail disappeared in the blur of heat which made the sky shiver like quicksilver. Sandra heaved a sigh of relief. Perhaps they would leave her alone now.

Bellies bulging, the horses had been willing enough to leave the waterhole since there was no forage except for mesquite and thorny cacti. The lead mare had stepped out briskly, and Sandra had been able, with some initial hard riding, to keep her heading out across the desert.

Within a few hours, however, heads began to droop, hooves to drag in the sand. Then, time and again, Sandra had to push Brandy into headlong gallop to keep the kinks out of the slender thread of horses as first one horse and then another bulged away from the line of march in an attempt to return to the waterhole.

The merciless glaring sun burned right through Sandra's sweat-stained shirt. It dried her face until she could feel the skin pinching her cheekbones, feel her lips crack despite the fact that she kept raising the canteen to moisten them.

Rimrock Red, no match in endurance with the sinewy, tendon-tough mustangs, trailed farther and farther behind the main column. The foals all lost their friskiness and sought to quench their thirst by suckling mares who gave them sharp nips and body-jolting thumps with back hooves sharply lifted.

One little paint mare, obviously with foal, was having an unusually difficult time. Sandra hoped the foal would not be born out here on the desert, that the little paint wouldn't go into labor until they had reached safety.

The urge the horses felt to return to the waterhole sometimes became epidemic. Sandra was riding the swift little cutting horse into the ground and she knew it. No sooner would she turn one horse back into the line of march than another would try to break away.

All around the desert vegetation was thinning, and such plants as there were became dwarfed. The prickly-pear cactus armed against any intruder, the creosote bush with its own chemicals to block invasions of other plant species, the occasional desert willow sprig marking some long, dry arroyo — these disappeared, and then for as far as she could see there was nothing but the harsh whiteness of alkaline flats.

It was a country of neither sand nor earth. It was a country where the dragging hooves failed to raise even a breath of dust. It was a glaring white land of intense burning avoided by all desert animals and, Sandra suspected, avoided by even God Himself.

Her map indicated that it was about fifteen miles across — four hours if a man walked briskly, maybe two hours if a horse had the energy to canter that far, but an eternity if the sun had already taken its toll of life-supporting juices, if the harsh, dry air had shriveled skin to the texture of sandpaper, if the muscles — man's or animal's — were limpid as spaghetti which had already endured the scalding.

But it was there, astride the route to the mountains, a merciless Styx, that mystical river which guards hell, and so if you wanted to get out of hell there was no way but to cross it.

The hammerheaded mare pawed the white crust, whinnied fearfully and looked back. Sandra imagined she could see the sharp whinny run through the rest of the herd like a thin, invisible thread of fear.

This would never do. She looked to her lasso, kicked Brandy in the ribs, and riding up swiftly alongside the mare cracked the coiled rope across her bony hips.

"Hiya!" her voice cracked with the effort. "Hiya!" She turned Brandy, circled, and coming up, again cracked the mare.

Slowly then the gangly horse shuffled forward. Just as slowly the rest of the herd followed.

A hundred yards and the lead mare stopped. At once the rest of the horses stopped and dropped their heads. Sandra rode back along-side the hammerheaded one and struck her re-peatedly. Once again she moved off, this time at a shuffling trot, but after a hundred feet she was walking again, except this time the whistle of the rope being twirled in the air kept her walking.

An hour, two . . . three, and then the herd was no longer moving but had bunched up and huddled around the lead mare and the white stallion — all except Rimrock and the little paint mare far to the rear with heads hanging so low their muzzles touched the acrid alkaline surface.

Once, twice . . . five times the girl charged the band of huddled horses to get them moving again. Each time they exploded in slow motion in all directions, but as soon as she left they came like iron filings back to the magnetic lead mare.

Sandra bit her lower lip, pulled down the brim of her hat and concentrated her charge on the lead mare. But this time the mare eluded her, and breaking into a trot headed straight back toward the waterhole where they had spent the night. The other horses sensed her intent, and a chorus of whinnies announced *their* intentions. They began to trot east, following the bony one, back across the miles which had been won, back across the alkaline flats, along the torturous trail they had just traveled, back to where there was water waiting. When the herd shuffled past Rim-rock he raised his head as if in amazement.

Sandra got down. She knew she couldn't stop them. Taking her canteen, she stood at Brandy's head and poured water into her hat and held it so the little cutting horse could drink. Then she took the reins in her right hand and began to walk. When she passed Rimrock, he fell in behind. When she passed the pitiful little paint with her bulging belly, she followed on along.

So they moved, a dispirited girl and three dispirited horses. And a buzzard came and circled so high it was a black pinprick in the white heat of the sky. Within minutes the retreating herd had gone so far it looked like a shimmering mirage. In another ten minutes the herd was lost from sight.

Sandra lowered her head, and deciding to conserve Brandy's strength, braced for the long walk. Underfoot the earth was hot as the sky above. On and on, along the plainly marked trail which the herd of horses had twice now gouged into the sand. Up the sandy slope, down a rocky draw. Cactus reaching out and stabbing. Lizards looking like arrogant dragons. More buzzards in the sky, but lower now, getting ready to play their gruesome role in the inevitable chain of life. On and on and on . . .

16

The last miles Sandra walked oblivious of her surroundings. Only when Brandy broke away and began running did she know she was near the waterhole. At the edge of the hole she fell and rolled down the bank. Half in and half out of the water she lay there while Rimrock and Brandy, only a few feet away, stood drinking.

It had long been dark. There was only the light of the stars bright in the sky and brighter still in the waterhole. To save her horse, she had walked every torturous mile with heat from the sand burning right through the soles of her boots.

Finally she sat up. She could see the horses, scattered and looking for food. Bending forward she splashed water over her head and face.

Gradually she felt her strength return. She stood, grasped Brandy's reins, and led her away from the water.

She took off the saddle, the bridle, and slipped on a halter. Then she slumped back to the ground, and with the hard saddle for a pillow she fell asleep.

The horses slept too, shifting weight from leg to leg, and never noticed when a rattlesnake visited the waterhole and, in the light of the moon which had risen, almost caught a kangaroo rat.

Morning came. Though the horses moved restlessly, Sandra still slept. Then it was the airplane which finally awakened her. There it was, and there was the sun too, and Sandra couldn't decide which of the two she hated most.

The plane, once again well out of rifle range, cruised back and forth, a buzzard waiting like all the rest for the end. Sandra shaded her eyes to watch it, and she wondered why it had come since it showed no inclination to come down to attack.

Surely the pilot had other things to do than waste gas merely to taunt her. Then it dawned on her. The horse killers were only biding their time. They probably believed that she wouldn't be foolhardy enough to try crossing the desert with an unruly gang of wild mustangs. Or, if she did try, they must have figured the horses would run away from her, come back to the prairie.

And they had been right. The horses had come back. And now, when they became hungry enough, they would again retrace their steps, retreat farther, until this time they would be grazing knee-deep in the prairie grasses from which they'd first been driven.

It would only be a matter of time then. They would know for a certainty that she would ultimately have to ride for supplies. Once gone, the pilot would start the herd toward Three Bends, and along the way the men in jeeps would close in to finish the job.

Tears of anger started up in her eyes. She got to her feet and shook a fist at the gleaming, silver airplane. Then she shouted, "You can't do it. I tell you, you can't do it."

The horses, startled at the sound of a human voice, all lifted their heads and looked in her direction. "You can't do it!" she shouted again, and then she slumped down beside the saddle feeling crumpled and crushed because she knew they could do it, because the horse killers had calculated correctly.

When Sandra looked up again the plane turned and in moments melted away into the dancing white heat.

She went to the waterhole and, taking off all her clothes, slipped into the water. Then with sand she scrubbed her body until it turned red, and her courage came back on her racing blood, and by the time she was dry again, she was ready for breakfast.

Her supplies were dwindling. Spreading packets of dehydrated food on the sand, she counted and estimated she had enough remaining for four days. Fortunately there was still about seven pounds of oats. Brandy would need that if she was going to outlast the mustangs, and that was precisely what Sandra now had in mind.

As for Rimrock? His lot was cast with that of the wild ones. He'd have to measure up, make it on his own, because if she shared Brandy's oats with her red stallion, the little cutting mare would never have that edge of strength that she was going to need.

Then she got out the map, and with the pencil stub wrote in the margin:

"Fifth morning. July 2. Tried desert crossing. Horses aborted. Back at desert waterhole."

All day the herd hugged the waterhole. Sandra made a canopy by draping the saddle blanket between two clumps of cactus. Almost hourly she visited the waterhole, and in her clothes, soaked herself luxuriantly.

The horses became increasingly restless as night approached. They had been without food a night and a day. One more day, she figured, and their strength would be waning.

Fully expecting that from time to time the herd would try to begin a general exodus in the direction of the prairie, the girl kept Brandy saddled. Each time then, when a horse, or a knot of horses, drifted too far from the waterhole, she slowly nudged them back.

That night was a nightmare of chasing shadows. Never sleeping and never dismounting, she pursued every shadow as horses time and again tried to move out, to head east toward the prairie.

By morning she and the little mare were both exhausted. Measuring out a hatful of grain, she fed Brandy. Then she took off the saddle and tied the mare to a mesquite bush. Then she fed herself and fell asleep.

She never knew precisely how long she had slept, but when she awakened, the horses were gone. She jumped to her feet, and saw them, moving out across the undulating sands in a long, wavering line, heading toward their home range.

Not waiting to pull on boots or to saddle up, she jumped on Brandy and kicked her heels into the horse's belly. Brandy bolted forward with a grunt and, kicking up sand, overtook the herd.

Sandra reined Brandy right up alongside the lead mare. Turning the big gangling horse back toward the waterhole, she swung the loose ends of her reins down sharply across the mare's haunches. Surprised, the mare leaped forward, then moved away at a dead run.

Sandra swung Brandy about, pressed down hard on the rest of the herd, and with rein ends lashing left and right had them all running back toward the waterhole.

Then it was, while the thirsty horses were jostling one another for position at the waterhole, that the airplane came to pay its morning visit. The pilot came down so low Sandra started for the rifle which lay in its scabbard alongside the saddle. Just as she grabbed the gun, the plane lifted and, climbing for altitude, flew away.

She jammed the rifle back into the leather case and breathed a long sigh of relief. She knew she'd never be able to shoot no matter how much she had come to hate the man. But, of course, it would never do for the pilot to discover that. With no threat from the gun, she would surely have in time lost control of the herd.

Well, if all went as she now planned, the pilot wouldn't find the herd at the waterhole when he came back tomorrow. Tonight she would move them. Soon as the moon came up she would start the trek, and she was counting on their apathy, their lethargy brought on by many hours without food.

Looking out at the herd from her shaded place beneath the saddle blanket, she could see how the lack of nourishment was already obvious in the way they moved about — like horses in slow motion.

In the evening she would again feed Brandy a heaping hatful of grain to strengthen her for the night ahead. Then, if she had calculated correctly, by the time the moon escaped the horizon, the horses would have neither the will left to resist, nor the energy to do anything except plod wearily in whichever direction she chose to push them.

She had seen it happen with cattle rescued from snowdrifts after a storm. Two days without food and they stood with drooping heads and a rider and horse could move them in any direction. She had seen it with deer marooned by snows in a winter woods. A few days and it was possible to approach quite close while animals stood dumbly watching.

Already the horses were listless. There were only infrequent, almost inconsequential, thrusts by one horse or another in the direction of the prairie. Another day beneath the blazing sun would further weaken their desire to resist a desert crossing.

There was the danger, however, that some might collapse, not make it. She was particularly worried about the foals, about the little paint mare who was carrying a foal, but it was a chance she would have to take, a calculated risk.

But then, so did crossing the mountains and getting around the vineyards entail their own share of calculated risks. In the beginning, when she had been planning the trek, the desert crossing had seemed the easiest part of the journey. She remembered the plan had been to start in the morning, be halfway by nightfall, and then make the last, the more arduous part of the crossing, at night when the sun had set and conditions for travel were more satisfactory.

But it wasn't working out that way. The final part of the journey would be made with the blazing sun sucking up life's juices. But there was no help for that now.

The herd had to be moved or the young, the old, the weak wouldn't make it.

During the afternoon Sandra dozed, came awake, dozed — a dozen times. During wakeful moments she imagined herself sitting by the tiny campfire with the bewhiskered professor, hearing him say, ". . . horses or sparrows. Eskimos or Englishmen . . . If everyone did the right thing . . ."

Then she would once again feel her sometimes wavering resolve to complete the journey strengthened. It had worried her each time she found herself vacillating as the temptation to go back to the comforts of the ranch rose up almost to overwhelm her.

Night came abruptly to the desert as it does at sea. She fed Brandy, fed herself, and then saddled up. Before mounting, she got out the map and wrote:

"Sixth night. July 3. Moon up we go. This time all the way or bust."

Astride the mare, she stationed herself to the east of the herd, the route back to the prairie, and once again alternately dozed and came awake, but this time while sitting in the saddle.

Soon as the moon rose, soon as it was high enough to sort out individual horses from the herd, she decided to move them. Instead of coming down on the huddled band with a whoop and a holler, she quietly, almost gently, infiltrated the herd, getting first one and then another horse to move west.

It was a long, slow process but eventually she had them moving, and when the direction to be taken became obvious, the hammerheaded mare stepped out from the little band and led the way.

This time there was a minimum of resistance. The horses seemed almost glad to be moving, regardless of the direction. Perhaps instinctively they knew that whichever course they took it must ultimately lead to grass.

Twice the lead mare did try to execute wide, swinging turns to maneuver the herd back in the direction of the prairie, but each time in a quiet and deliberate manner, Sandra turned the horse back so it was facing west, walking deeper and deeper into the desert.

Then at last the horses, strung out in a long line, were completely obedient to the quiet but relentless pressure of a suntanned girl in long pigtails sitting high on a little bay horse which stayed alert for straying forms, ready even without a command to spurt forward and bring back in line a recalcitrant marcher.

The sun rose with a blinding light to announce its intentions of making this another burning day, but by then they were already halfway across the alkaline flats.

17

That morning the airplane did not come. That morning the mountains with their grassy foot-hills, their flowing streams, their cool meadows, loomed shadowy and enticingly above the western horizon — seemingly near but never, it seemed, coming closer.

Step after weary step and still the mountains were as distant as when they had first material-ized through the simmering haze. Mile after mile, hour after hour. It was an agonizing ex-perience to see the shadowy refuge, to know it was there, but to know also that some, perhaps many of the horses might not have the strength, under the searing sun, to make it.

The line of march became longer and longer

as stragglers fell farther and farther behind. Several times Sandra rode to the head of the line and, getting out ahead of the lead mare, tried to slow her pace. The old horse seemed glad to slow down, and sometimes she stopped and stood still.

The other horses, instead of continuing to walk and close the gaps in the long line of march, stopped too. Riding off to one side Sandra surveyed the procession and guessed she had horses strung out for a quarter of a mile.

Bringing up the rear was Rimrock and the little paint mare with bulging belly. Never having had his stamina tested, Rimrock did not have the reserve of toughness which made it possible for the wiry mustangs to survive blizzards and droughts, outlast onslaughts of disease and parasitic invasions. As for the little mare, it seemed as if she might drop her foal at any moment.

In the wilds, nature cracked the whip. So Sandra knew that even though the herd was no blue-ribbon sampling of horseflesh, underneath they were all rawhide-tough — the end result of nature's law under which only the fittest survive.

So she rode to the end of the line to prod Rimrock to greater effort. But there was no prodding him. He moved like a mechanical horse, putting one hoof slowly in front of the other as if the effort took considerable deliberation.

Just ahead of Rimrock was the little paint and then a black mare with a bay filly having four white socks and a diamond blaze. The mare seemed reasonably strong, but the filly was faltering, staggering.

Sandra had heard stories about the desert sun, and how men afoot and without water never lasted through the second day. And now she could believe it. She could see the horses wilting minute by minute.

If they had been provided grass, she was sure the herd would have had little trouble crossing the desert. But now they had been without food too long, and their reserves of strength, their resistance melted as the sun soaked up their juices.

Finally the mare with the faltering foal stopped. The youngster's head went between the mother's legs as the filly tried to suckle. When no milk came, the filly thumped the mare's belly impatiently with her head, and a thin little whinny, like a child's scream for help, escaped her.

The mother moved again. The whole wild band, never trying to turn back now that the mountains up ahead beckoned them, moved like a wavering mirage in the film of heat dancing across the desert.

Rimrock and the little paint fell farther and farther behind. Sandra was tempted to pour some of what water remained in her canteen into her hat for them to drink. But she resisted the temptation. She might still need it. In the end the fate of the whole herd might depend on her determination literally to whip them the last mile.

Finally the little filly with the white blaze went down. The mare stood over the foal nudging her to arise, whinnying softly for her youngster to lift her head, get back on her feet. The foal tried, got up, staggered a few steps and went down again, her muzzle plowing into the hot alkaline earth.

A little cry of pain escaped Sandra. She jumped from the saddle and went to kneel beside the downed foal. The mare moved a few paces off and stood staring dumbly while Sandra tried to get the filly back on her feet.

It was no use. Going to where Brandy waited spraddle-legged, Sandra got her canteen and going back to the foal wet a hand to rub the young one's dry nostrils. It was like touching the rasping surface of sandpaper. The foal licked greedily at the moisture, and Sandra, pulling out a kerchief, soaked it and gave it to the filly to suck.

"That's all. No more," she said, as if the filly might understand.

Then when Sandra got off her knees to return the canteen to the pommel of the saddle, the filly got to her feet and tried to follow, but went down again. Sandra picked her up, and holding her belly muscles tight against the load, lifted and pushed until the filly was stretched across the saddle.

Whipping out her knife, she cut two lengths from her rope and looping each — one around the front legs and the other around the rear fetlocks — tied the filly fast to the saddle.

Taking the remainder of the rope, she walked

back to where Rimrock stood spraddle-legged. She tied one end of the rope to his halter and the other end to Brandy's saddle strap.

Then on foot, filly in the saddle, Rimrock in tow, she hurried Brandy so as to catch up with the herd and prod the stragglers to greater effort.

It was noon when they left the alkaline flats. Here desert plants grew. But still with unrelenting fury the sun scorched a path down the afternoon sky. No lizards or any horned toads showed themselves, and the desert seemed deserted and desolate except for a waiting convoy of buzzards which soared now in an expectant flock of birds all obviously certain that soon the sun would serve them an ample feast of horseflesh.

Sandra guessed it had been about six hours since the mountains first came into view on the horizon. She couldn't believe that they seemed as distant now as they had when she first saw them. As they walked, four more horses, another mare with colt, and another paint and the gray, dropped back to the rear of the column. Sandra urged them along by flapping her hat across their haunches and almost mechanically chanting, "Hey! Hey! Get along there! Get along there!"

Of all the horses she was amazed to see that the strongest was the old lead mare. Hardly more than a rack of bones to begin with, she plodded on mechanically as though powered by springs instead of a heart that surely by now must be tiring.

Even the white stallion wasn't doing as well as the lead mare for all his seemingly great strength, even considering his powerful muscles, which still bulged with each painful step. Gone now, of course, was the stallion's concern about servicing the harem, and he plodded among them only another horse with a hanging head.

"If I can only keep them going until dark maybe we can make it," Sandra kept saying to herself.

Though the nights had not been cool, with the sun gone the heat might be bearable. Daytime temperatures on the desert were capable of rising above hundred and twenty degrees in the shade, and, of course, there was no shade. She knew that in the sun it was hot enough to fry an egg on a rock in a matter of seconds.

Now, her feet burning, her eyes reddened and sore enough to induce a perpetual squint, she wondered if they would ever walk beneath trees, among cool grasses beside the watery wealth of a cold mountain stream.

The foal, hanging over the saddle, had at first lifted its head and convulsed its body to be free of such restraints as kept it such an unusual prisoner. But now it had ceased struggling and hung limply, its eyes closed.

Rimrock became more and more of a burden, and sometimes Brandy was literally pulling the red stallion through the sand, and Sandra was pulling Brandy.

Having to take a drink more often now, Sandra, even as she walked, permitted herself the luxury of a face wash with a dampened palm.

The water evaporated even before she could feel it, so she decided against enjoying such an extravagance.

Putting one foot in front of the other, her eyes on the hot sands, Sandra walked with bent head, swerving only when a reaching cactus jabbed needlelike thorns into her hide.

Her thoughts wandered sometimes. Then she would be home at the ranch sitting on the long front porch enjoying a dish of velvety-smooth, deliciously cool ice cream while a breeze played down from the foothills to set little dust devils spinning and dancing across the yard.

Or she would be in the shadowy cool students' lounge at the university after a fast game of tennis with a tall beer spilling icy white suds down the sides of a frosted glass, and the jukebox would be wailing softly in another room where the students sometimes danced.

Or she would be a very small child again playing in the buff under the spreading cottonwood, taking refreshing plunges in the sweet water which an artesian well poured into the concrete horse tank.

Her nostrils were raw now as the dry hot air irritated and ruptured some of the tiny blood vessels.

Her reverie, her dreamworld collapsed as she bumped hard into the gray ahead, who had stopped suddenly. Staggering back a few steps, she whipped off her hat, and thumping the gray with it, got the animal moving again.

Then she looked up at the mountains and was surprised that she could pick out detail: a precipitous and shining white cliff; a lone pine, tall and sentinel-like on a cleared slope which had either been lumbered or burned; the low-lying cottonwoods, fringe of the forest; a canyon, dark shadowy crease back into the face of the hills . . .

Suddenly the pace quickened. It was almost imperceptible but it was enough for Sandra to notice. Then a horse neighed anxiously. Another tried to whinny but managed only a whimper. Then the lead mare broke into a tottering, stumbling trot. The rest of the herd followed at its ragged best, the long line of horses swaying and squirming across the desert sands like a great, disjointed snake.

Water! Sandra thought. They must have smelled water!

Brandy started ahead and Sandra had to dig in her heels to hold her. Even Rimrock showed a glimmer of life. His pace quickened as he tried to match the fevered surge of the little cutting horse to whom he was tied.

Only the foal did not respond. Hanging like dead, the filly bounced as Brandy cavorted and reared to be free of the girl and off and away to a cooling drink.

So Sandra dropped the reins, grabbed the rope which tied Brandy to Rimrock, and then as it slid blistering through her hands, she got out her knife and cut the rope a foot short of where it was tied to the stallion's halter.

Then in a staggering, sand-gouging rush the long line of horses, including Brandy still burdened with the unconscious foal, moved out and away. When the lead mare, head high now, breasted the first grasses which marked the fringe of cottonwoods, Sandra was alone in the desert.

A smile hurting her cracked lips, Sandra looked up at the buzzards and shouted, "Fooled ya! Didn't we! Fooled ya!" Then she too broke into a sand-scuffling trot to come to the cool greenery.

Part Three

18

The stream was wide and moved placidly through tall, sparse grasses at the point where Sandra finally caught up with the herd, all knee-deep in the water.

Permitting herself a hasty, deliciously cool but quiet submersion in the stream, she ran to where Brandy was drinking and grabbing her bridle literally hauled her out of the small river.

With the cutting horse in tow, she caught up Rimrock, and though the two horses fought to get back to the water, she managed to tether both to a fallen log.

Perhaps the mustangs might luxuriate in the icy stream and drink to their stomachs' content without getting sick, but Sandra was sure that such a gorging would most certainly cause the little cutting horse and her red stallion to founder.

Sandra cut the foal's bonds and lowered the little animal from Brandy's saddle to the ground. The filly's eyes were open and glazed. Sandra felt for the artery in the neck but there was no pulse.

Salvaging her rope ends, Sandra dragged the tiny filly up and away from the stream onto a smooth, bare rock. Then she looked up at the hovering buzzards and said, "It's the only one you'll get, damn you!"

Some of the horses had already finished drinking when Sandra went to the stream and drank from it. Then she went to where she had tied Rimrock and Brandy and unsaddled the cutting horse and then let both horses go back to the stream to finish drinking. By then the other horses had already scattered, and some had begun to nibble on the harsh, sour grass which grew from the infertile gravel banks which held in the river.

Now it was her turn. She shed her clothes, loosed the ribbons which bound her hair in pigtails and submerged her aching body into the water. A series of tremors convulsed her, and she backed out of the water. She realized the danger of going into shock by remaining submerged too long, a condition icy water can produce in those whom the sun has dehydrated.

When the sun had once more warmed her, she reentered the stream, but cautiously this time — knee-deep first, then to her buttocks, and finally when the water was high as her navel she merely stood half in and half out of the water, letting the skin absorb moisture, and letting the burning cactus cuts on her legs go numb.

After a while she splashed water high as her breasts, and then when the shock of that wore off, she scooped the glistening river so water cascaded over her shoulders.

Then she lunged forward and dived beneath the surface, and holding her breath swam underwater almost to the center of the river. She burst forth gasping, and with smooth but powerful strokes swam back to shore.

Coming up the bank she went to where her clothes were piled, and slipped into her boots. Then, still naked, she rounded up Brandy and led her a little way back from the stream and slipped a rope halter on her.

She turned at once back to the fringe of thin grass along the river. Rummaging in a sack, she came up with a bar of soap. Where her clothes were piled she kicked out of her boots, and then went back in the stream, where she lathered her hair and body and rinsed it a half-dozen times before she felt satisfied.

Then she gathered her clothes, and sitting naked on a flat rock, began to scrub them. When they had been soaped and rinsed she spread them out in the sun on the white stones.

She rummaged through her gear and found some figs and dates, and a chocolate bar which had melted and leaked into the saucepan. She ate the fruit, dug out the chocolate with a forefinger and sucked it into her mouth. Then she went back to the river for another drink.

Standing on the shore she surveyed the herd.

They were eating the grass, but with little relish. She would have to find pasture. For now that could wait.

She and the animals had recuperated swiftly. She stretched her lithe young body upward toward the sun. Then she went to where her saddle spanned a log, and rummaging through the gear came up with a hairbrush.

She found a spot in the shade of a huge boulder where a little breeze came up from the water to caress her, and brushed her hair until it was smooth and silken.

19

The temptation was to sit naked in the shade of the big rock all day, but she knew she had to find good grass or the herd would wander off on its own to seek better rations. Then too, there was the matter of the little filly, bloating already in the hot sun, and the great black birds circling lower and lower until she knew at last even with her present, they would not be denied, and she didn't want to see it happen.

So with the sun near the horizon, she dressed, caught up Brandy, saddled her, and began the roundup.

The trek was upstream, and in the beginning it was arduous because the horses split and some walked one side of the river while the others stayed on the other side.

Crossing and recrossing the river — sometimes swimming the little horse — she kept the herd pointed upstream toward where cottonwoods and trembling aspen edged the foothills beyond which were the stands of mountain pine.

The meadow she had only been wishing for appeared abruptly. She was passing through a dense thicket of aspen when suddenly there it was, such a wealth of good grass as was enough to make a rancher's pulse race and which brought the hungry horses forward at an anxious gallop.

There must have been more than a hundred acres of tender, knee-high grass interspersed with small groves of young aspen whose leaves sighed in the breeze and twinkled in the setting sun.

Sandra could not understand the presence of such an Eden. Before turning Brandy free to fill her belly, she continued to ride upstream to determine, if possible, what might be responsible for this green richness.

The mystery was quickly solved. Remnants of what had once been a mile-long beaver dam were marked by decaying logs and branches — a welter of them where once the dam stretched across from one plateau to another. At one time the beavers had so successfully dammed the little river that water had fed back and out and around into hundreds of aspen groves, prime forage for the furry industrialists.

The dam had been kept in good repair for many years. Years of eutrophication had likely settled a thick and rich layer of fertile debris on the pond bottom. Then likely a trapper came along, decimated the beaver colony, and when there were no longer enough laborers at the dike, a spring freshet or a flash flood had knocked out the structure and the cascading waters had spread the accumulated fertility of the pond bottom, leaving a rich layer of topsoil hungry to grow good grasses.

She would make her headquarters near the old dam, she decided, in a grove of aspen. From there she could look out in all directions on the pasture nature had created. Brandy, reluctant to keep her head up, was turned loose to join in the feasting. Then she stood to look at her herd of horses, headless it seemed, as they grazed with ears below the grassline, tails twitching from flank to flank as if in ecstasy.

Making camp was a quick thing. The thin rain poncho first, and then the saddle blanket spread on the green grass would be her bed. The saddle was tilted a little to provide a pillow. Gear and food, what little was left of it, were lined along a log. A place for a fire was cleared of grass and lined with white stones from the river, and the canteen was filled with water and hung from an overhead limb where breezes might cool it.

The sun was down by the time she finished. She lighted a small fire, chewed on a few dates and then pulled out the map to make another entry along the margin:

"Seventh night. July 4. My Independence Day! Desert behind. Good grass. Wide river. Heaven."

Her next move would take some planning. But

it would have to wait. She hadn't slept in twenty-four hours. And the twenty-four hours prior to that had been a day of catnaps, often taken while sitting in the saddle. Then, even while she thought about it, her eyes closed, and with her head on the saddle, she fell soundly asleep.

All around her the horses continued to stuff their bellies. It wasn't until midnight that some lay down, and others slouched onto three legs to doze. It was a peaceful night, quiet except for the occasional snuffling of a horse, quiet except for the single coyote which just before dawn yelped that another day was coming.

The coyote awakened Sandra. At first she couldn't comprehend where she was. Then sitting up and looking around at the horses scattered in the clearing, she remembered. Getting up, she stretched, then headed for the river. Refreshed by the cool waters she came back, lighted a fire, and warmed moistened dehydrated beef. Looking up at the high peaks of the mountain range, she was reminded of the obstacles ahead.

If she hadn't known it before, the high peaks convinced her she couldn't cross except where the four-lane superhighway cut through at Brenner's Pass, and she had no idea how far away she was from the road.

As for supplies, she knew the town of Sago was along the highway near where the concrete began to lift to span the mountains. She'd have to find it to provide provisions for herself, and more oats for Brandy.

And the vineyards? They were on the other

side of the mountains. At this moment that was like being on the dark side of the moon. First things first, she thought. A trip to Sago. Then a look at the highway where it went climbing off into the mountains. Then . . . well, then, getting the herd off this grassy pasture and out onto the road hopefully to make a swift and safe crossing to the western slopes would be an ordeal of fast riding and expert maneuvering. She had confidence in Brandy. The little cutting horse seemed able to guess which way a recalcitrant marcher might like to turn and cut the mustang back into the herd.

But this day she would recuperate. This day was a time to let the strength seep back into her weary body, her worried mind. This day she'd take a head count of her horses, a closer look at the herd, which over the days had become not just another herd of wild animals, but an assortment of individuals with the strengths and weaknesses, beauty and ugliness, little deceits and little eccentricities typical of a like assortment of human beings.

She had even begun to name them. There was the old lead mare, and she was Grandma. And, of course, there was the magnificent white stallion. Every time she looked at him the name Cossack leaped into her mind. Then there was the walleyed horse, her pinkish-white eyes shining even in the evening gloom, and in Sandra's mind she was Spook.

Then there was a bony old bay mare who was always sticking her nose into every other horse's business, and Sandra called her Knuckles. The yearling stallion who kept grunting and moaning around the mares she named Romeo. The most striking of the paints was Injun. A black with an old hip injury that gave her a peculiar gait became Stumble.

She observed and began to sort out the pecking order and the little cliques, the societies within the society.

Then if she began to feel a family familiarity with them, so too the horses, most members of the herd, by now had come to accept her presence. If they moved off when she approached, it was never far, and sometimes, especially if she was mounted on Brandy, they permitted her alongside. Then if their ears were laid back momentarily, they soon seemed to forget her presence and got on with their grazing.

At noon Sandra opened a packet of dehydrated potatoes and, with what was left of the morning beef, made a stew. Then she slept.

Awakening a half hour later, she sat up abruptly, but then relaxed when she saw the horses scattered down along the river. Pulling on her boots, she walked to the old beaver dam, and where the rushing waters had jammed together an interlocked pile of aspen logs, she climbed to the top of the jam and began a head count.

Counting Rimrock, she could locate only thirty horses. According to her calculations there should have been thirty-two. Then she remembered the dead foal, but the count was still one short. She counted again, and then a third time. Now she was certain that one horse was missing.

So she began to sort out the animals in her mind. In a flash it dawned on her. The little paint mare, the one she had been afraid might drop a foal while crossing the desert, was missing.

It made sense. The horse had probably gone off to have her foal. Somewhere right now, perhaps in an aspen grove, perhaps a little higher up among the pines, she was stretched out straining to bring life out from the darkness of her womb.

Once with foal she'd probably drift quickly back to the meadow, the only place grassy enough to feed a nursing mother.

Horses on the range preferred to leave the herd when they foaled. Sometimes they might stay away for days, even weeks, before returning to the fold. Except here the circumstances were different, and Sandra was not concerned. Within days the foal would be strong enough to trot alongside its mother down to the road, up the median strip, over the mountains.

Clambering down from the logjam, she walked down among the horses. They moved slowly out of her way, and when she had come to where Rimrock was sleeping on three legs, she gave a low whistle. He came to her just as he had before the critical day in the pole corral when he had sent Gerald Deever and his syringe of curare flying and almost trampled the man's head into the dust in the bargain.

While Rimrock nuzzled her, Cossack, a couple of hundred yards off, stood head high, ears alert, watching.

Sandra wondered what must be going through the white stallion's mind. Did he sense that between herself and Rimrock there was a special relationship? She doubted it.

Slapping Rimrock across the flank, she sent him off on a fun run which ended with a series of stiff-legged joyous bucks.

Tomorrow she would ride him.

20

The sun, dropping behind the mountains by mid-afternoon, put the grassy pasture into such an early shade that by suppertime she was glad for the crackling fire. Finishing the stew left over from lunch, and munching dates and figs, she watched the darkness gather in the lowlands and ascend the mountains until only the peaks still glowed, reflections from a sun which hours before had left the western sky.

But it was not dark for long. Up out of the prairie, up out of the desert, an amber moon turned quickly white, and she could see the shadows of the horses scattered below among the young aspen groves, along the silvery, shining river.

Once again she got out the map and wrote:

"Eighth night. July 5. Happy and holding."

The last thing she remembered before falling asleep was an anxious whinny, a cry almost of pain, but her eyes closed anyway and when next she opened them the sun was already drying the dew crystals in her hair.

She had no choice of rations for this morning's breakfast. There was only one packet of potatoes and eight dates left. While she ate the potatoes, made pasty with river water, and permitted herself four of the remaining eight dates, her eyes searched the herd for the pregnant paint mare.

After breakfast she climbed to the top of the logjam for a better look, but the little horse was not back with the herd.

There was no helping that situation today. She'd have to ride. Four dates would not exactly a dinner make. Now that she was relaxing for the first time in many days, her hunger was becoming a thing to be reckoned with.

She had decided she would ride Rimrock — if she could catch him. Belly full again, the red stallion was scouting the mares, and Cossack was not far behind him.

Quite by accident she came upon him while he was enamored of a bay mare who was flicking her tail flirtatiously. In one jump she had him by the halter. When he began to rear and plunge, she talked him into standing, if not passively, then at least quietly enough so in soothing tones she could rekindle memories of their ranch days — long rides, gloriously comforting grooming sessions.

Finally allowing himself to be led, she brought

the horse back to her camp and with a rope end tied him to a bush. The bush would bend if he made up his mind to turn tail and return to the mare, whereas a rope, tied to anything rigid as a tree, would break.

The horse wanted no part of the bit, so Sandra let him have a sharp flat hand slap across the nose, and then the iron bar was rattling between his teeth. The saddle blanket made him shiver, but when the saddle was plopped into place, he cavorted and she turned him hard up against a tree.

She kept him against the tree and leaped into the saddle. When her weight came down into the stirrups, he trembled again.

Then he stood as if shocked, but when he felt her knee he whirled, almost unseating her, and then took off at a clumsy trot among the stones.

At the river edge he went down to his knees in a jumble of rocks, but with the bridle she yanked him up, and then he was more careful picking his way downstream, out of the green pasture, between the shale outcroppings and around the armed cactus, until at last they hit level land.

Then there was no holding him, and after a series of jolting bucks, he leveled off and with neck and head stretched forward, he streaked away. Sandra lifted a little in the stirrups, leaned forward, and let him go.

Her black hair streamed from beneath the broad brim of her hat, and she narrowed her eyes to keep the wind from starting a flash flood of stinging tears.

Unafraid now, she gave herself over to being a part of the animal. She felt his strength and it became her strength. She felt his unutterable joy at being allowed to run full gallop, and she found his muscles with her knees and melted her body into his effort until she felt she was another moving muscle, part of the racing horse.

He ran straight out into the desert. Slowly she began to turn him back toward the foothills. He turned grudgingly, a wide swing that sent sand flying, mesquite bending, cactus snapping away as if on pencil stems.

Only when the land began to rise could she slow him down.

By the time the incline of the earth became more abrupt, he was satisfied to settle back with a grunt into a crow-hopping walk.

The incline continued to increase sharply upward and Rimrock began plodding. In a little while, when she climbed down he seemed glad to be rid of the burden and walked nicely on lead.

At the bottom of a butte, the highest promontory around, she tied the horse. Then on foot she began seeking boot and handholds to get to the top.

It was a breathtaking, arduous climb. Sometimes she could only inch her way along, finding a toehold here, a fingerhold in another place. Then sometimes where winds had found a crevice to widen, she could climb swiftly in the eroded path. Up and up until her gloved hands clutched the rim. With a final grunt she completed the arduous climb and pulled herself out onto the butte and lying flat on her stomach, gasped for air.

Wind recovered, she sat up to look around. To the west were more buttes rising to be married to the mountains. To the north she could make out the green postage stamp of her temporary home, the pasture. To the east stretched the desert.

Then to the south she saw what she was looking for, a cloud of haze on the horizon. It had to be Sago. Smoke from the smelters would account for the haze. It was ten miles anyway, maybe twenty, perhaps even thirty. In the clear air, with nothing but flat prairie and desert in between, there was no way of judging distance.

She knew Sago. It was a small mining town. Silver mostly, a hard-bitten little town getting as much of its revenue from the tourists who followed the superhighway west as from the two worked-out mines. Maybe four thousand people lived there, but the stores would have the provisions she needed.

Relaxed now, she sat clutching her knees and sucking at her underlip, which had been cut by a sliver of rock.

She looked at her watch. It was eleven o'clock. Rimrock was strong. So maybe she should ride today, get it over with.

She had no water. She had no sacks in which to bring back the provisions. Sacks she could come by. But water? She licked her already dry lips, and thought, Well, if it's ten miles I can make it in less than two hours without pushing. If it's twenty miles, she'd have to hold the horse down to go the distance — probably walk most of the way. She'd never do it under four hours.

Still, what was the use in postponing it? With Rimrock she felt certain, no matter the distance, she could make it by nightfall. Then they could ride back by moonlight or just bed down somewhere en route.

Short rations had already tightened her belly. Then there had been the brief headaches, certain warning of more consequences if she didn't eat with some degree of regularity.

The climb down turned into a back-blistering slide. She slowed herself with feet and hands and she was glad for the gloves. Her abrupt appearance in a final body-tobogganing drop landed her right next to the horse and he began to fight the lead line with which she had tied him to a bush.

"Easy, boy," she cautioned. "Easy now." She quietly talked him out of the jitters. Then she got up, rubbed her sore behind, and untying the horse, swung aboard.

Out on the flatlands Rimrock fell into a smooth and rhythmical ground-eating canter to which she could accommodate herself as easily as if she'd been sitting in a rocking chair.

An hour later she could see the haze in the sky from her low ground position. Another half hour and she could see the silhouettes of the smokestacks. Then in another half hour they were walking along dusty roads between dilapidated shacks of corrugated iron and adobe houses — through small crowds of milling children and barking dogs, and around small knots of adults who viewed her and the horse with curiosity and amusement.

A supermarket was her objective. Only there could she hope to find fast-frozen dehydrated food products — the kind of rations which would take her the most miles hauling the least weight.

She was likely to find a supermarket downtown but she doubted the wisdom of taking Rimrock into traffic. She hadn't seen a horse anywhere, and doubted if the people of Sago owned any.

At a dilapidated gas station where a sign dangled from one brace and the plaster had come away from the walls of the building in great chunks, she asked the young Mexican attendant if she could tether her horse out back for an hour.

"Help yourself," the young man said, grinning. "In three years," he went on, chuckling, "nobody has asked to stable a horse here, and now I get two in one day."

Sandra smiled. "Well, business must be picking up," she said.

"That kind of business I don't need," the young man said.

Dismounting she led Rimrock around to the back of the building. She found a burro, not a horse, tied to a length of old snow fencing behind which lurked ancient hulks of defunct automobiles.

Leaving a considerable distance between Rimrock and the burro, Sandra tied the horse. Then entering the station she tried the rest room door.

It was locked. Beside the grimy window of the station she saw a Coke machine. She dropped coins in the slot, heard a tinkle followed by the dull thud of a falling bottle. She picked up the icy bottle and popping it open, let the cool, delightful liquid rush down to assure her pinched stomach that things were looking better.

She finished the Coke and was starting on a second when the rest room door opened and before she could turn, she heard a voice say, "Why, Miss Bradford, I thought you were somewhere out on the desert."

Turning, she found herself looking into the twinkling, amused eyes of Dr. Paul Pelham.

When she could find no quick way of saying how glad she was to see him, she said, "Of course, Dr. Pelham, I should have recognized Bessie."

"Oh, then you've already said hello to Bessie."

"I've got my horse tied back there."

"Get across the desert?"

Sandra nodded.

"Any casualties?"

"One filly."

"Here to shop?"

Again Sandra nodded.

"Well, so am I — after a fashion. Usually I take enough along for at least six weeks. But when a rattlesnake spooked Bessie, she threw a pack."

"But how could that hurt the food?"

"Didn't. But my brandy was smashed, and if there's anything . . . well . . ."

Sandra smiled. "Where are you going to shop?" she asked.

"Right downtown."

"Well, I was going downtown to look for a supermarket."

"Shall we go then?" Dr. Pelham asked.

Sandra nodded.

As they walked away from the station, Dr. Pelham turned and said to the somewhat bewildered Mexican youth, "If you water and take good care of those two noble steeds back of your establishment there's a five-spot in it for you."

The boy's grin widened, and the bewhiskered old man and the tired, dirty, but happy girl went on toward where they could hear the arguing of autos.

21

While they were gorging on tacos, fried beans, and Coca-Cola, Sandra told Dr. Pelham about the desert crossing, about the green, grassy meadow she had found.

"Of course," he said, "I know about the meadow. I'm not more than six miles above it where a feeder creek comes down to join the river. We're practically neighbors."

As she sat there Sandra's spirits seemed suddenly to lift. More devastating than even the desert sun had been the feeling of being the last person on earth driving a herd of maverick horses across what had seemed like an endless desert in a deserted world. And now, she thought, I have a neighbor.

While in town she called home. Mrs. Webley answered. "Your father's worried," she said. "I think he plans to look for you. Where are you at?"

"But he can't. I don't want him to. Everything's fine now. I'm across the desert and in Sago picking up supplies."

"Well, I'll tell him," Mrs. Webley said, "but you know your father."

"Indeed I do," Sandra said, "and so do you. So please, please tell him not to spoil it now."

Mrs. Webley laughed softly. "Okay. You know I can handle it. He'll stay home — that is, if you promise to be careful."

"I will. I will," Sandra insisted.

Before she hung up then, Sandra felt the urge to tell Mrs. Webley how much she really meant in both the lives of herself and her father. She wanted to tell her how much she loved her, but she couldn't find the words.

When the receiver was back on the hook, she wondered if she could call her college roommate, Clarise. But what would she say? Clarise would never understand, not in a million years. She was a New York girl come West. Sandra smiled to herself. The West, especially a university town, was not the West at all. The West was out here, on the prairie, in the desert, among the buttes.

Sandra thought of Jim. He was one of the best things that had happened to her at school. But she couldn't reach him. He was somewhere in the Tonnoca range with a forestry crew. The thought of Jim warmed her.

She looked through the glass of the phone booth. Dr. Pelham had turned in his chair and was watching her. She came through the door and went over to him.

"Ready?" he asked.

"Ready as I'll ever be."

They picked up their bundles and left the store.

At the edge of town they got their mounts, waved to the smiling gas station attendant with the five-dollar bill in his hand, and leading Rimrock and Bessie, walked down the dusty street.

The sun was low to the horizon as Sago disappeared in a shimmer of heat waves behind them. Both girl and man were still walking, and Rimrock pranced impatiently, irritated that he must slow his pace to that of the mincing burro.

"Maybe you'd better ride on," Dr. Pelham suggested. "I'll make it to your camp by morning; we can have breakfast together."

"Thanks, but I'll walk," the girl said.

"But your horse, he'll never be able to accommodate himself to Bessie's plodding."

Most of Sandra's provisions had been packed on the burro, because Pelham's few brandy bottles — well protected this time in layers of the Sago *Free Press* — took up so little room.

"How long will you be staying in the meadow?" Dr. Pelham asked.

"I have to wait until the horses fill out a little, regain their strength. But I must go while there's still enough moon to make the highway drive by night."

"That's going to be a tricky drive," Pelham said.

"I know," Sandra replied. "It frightens me. Some horses might be killed, and then I would never forgive myself if a motorist was also injured or killed."

"Maybe I could help," Dr. Pelham said.

Sandra stopped walking. Her impatient horse ran into her. Looking over at the professor, she said, "I was hoping to do it on my own. Maybe it's childish, but it's something I have to prove — not only to myself, but also to my father."

Dr. Pelham tugged at his white beard. "So that's the way it is," he said. "I had suspected as much."

Sandra's cheeks flushed. "It's not that alone. The horses are my first concern. Primarily I'm doing it for them. But it is also my chance, an opportunity to prove . . . well . . ."

"No need to explain," Dr. Pelham interrupted. "Except I think — if the going gets too rough — that you remember that it is also an art, not only of politeness, but of wisdom, to know how to graciously accept, receive — help, companionship . . . A wise man once said, 'We gain as many friends by accepting favors as by giving them.' "

"I'll remember that," Sandra said.

"Please do, because you know I won't be far."

Rimrock's patience had petered out. He was dancing ahead of Sandra at the end of the reins, and even the placid Bessie was beginning to spook.

"Maybe I'll have to ride," Sandra finally said. "He'll have himself in a lather, and he's jerking my arms right out of my sockets."

"Think you can find the way in the dark?"

Sandra laughed. "I won't have to. With all those mares waiting back there, Rimrock will zero in on the meadow like a homing pigeon."

Dr. Pelham chuckled. "And that's a fact," he said. Sandra vaulted into the saddle and with a wave of her hand disappeared out across the sand, darkening now for its brief hiatus before the moon rose to chase the shadows.

Dr. Pelham was good as his word. He was on time for breakfast. Letting Bessie roam to graze, he did some wonderful things with pancake flour and bacon and coffee — mixed in tin cups and fried in a real frying pan that he took from his pack.

Sandra's black eyes twinkled appreciatively. "Delicious! Absolutely delicious!"

"You should try some of my pothole beans covered with bacon and molasses. It's the first thing I make after unpacking Bessie, and I let it simmer for days in the ground beneath the campfire ashes. It gets better and better and is always there hot and appetizing when I need a snack."

"You make my mouth water."

"Well, come on up some night. We'll have dinner together."

It was a signal for a laugh or at least a smile, but Sandra's mood had changed. "Something wrong?" Dr. Pelham asked.

"No, not really." Her smile was back. "It's just that I can't believe it's happening. That I'm driving a herd of wild horses across the mountains, and here I am sitting out in the nowhere with the famous Dr. Pelham."

"I think it's great," Pelham said. "It's probably the really last long wild horse drive of all time."

Sandra's face fell. "I only hope it comes off," she said.

"It will," the doctor said, piling tin cups into the frying pan for a trip to the river. "I've done some thinking on it. It'll come off." Sandra followed him down to the river.

Dishes scoured and packed, Dr. Pelham caught up Bessie's lead rope and started up the river.

"What are you going to do today?" he asked, turning to say good-bye.

"I have to find that paint mare. Though it isn't unusual for a mare due to foal to stay away a week or even two, I have a feeling something has gone wrong with her." She hesitated, then asked, "And what'll you be doing?"

"Sleep; perchance to dream."

Sandra laughed. "Come now," she said, "you can do better than Shakespeare."

"You flatter me now," Dr. Pelham said, "except honestly, I'm bushed."

It was then she remembered that he had walked through the night, while she, after a few short hours riding, had collapsed exhausted on her camp bed.

22

She watched for a long time until Dr. Pelham moved around a bend of the river and disappeared among the pines. Then she turned her attention to the horses. They were widely scattered, and there was no sign of the little paint.

Rimrock and Cossack were carrying on their interminable, long-range war. Each horse would graze briefly, and then abruptly lift his head to eye the other. Ears would lay back, the ground would be pawed, sometimes a warning whinny sounded — then back for a few more mouthfuls of grass. It was a standoff which must surely once again result in a confrontation involving flailing hooves and snapping teeth.

Brandy was far across the meadow standing with lowered head and probably sleeping. A few horses were stretched full length in the tall grass. Only their whisking tails betrayed their position.

She got out the map then, and since there was no room on any margins, turned the paper and wrote on the back:

"Tenth morning. July 7. Back from Sago with supplies."

Putting the map away, Sandra started for the old beaver dam, and climbed the logjam for a better look. She counted twice, and they were all there except for the little paint. Well, the pregnant mare had to be somewhere near, down probably in an aspen grove, probably already with foal or perhaps still waiting for birth.

But where to look? Certainly not on the best range. The mare would want to be away from the others. She must hunt the fringe of the meadow, going off into thickets and aspen, and cottonwood groves.

Systematically she began to circle the meadow, looking into all areas where trees afforded cover. She stood often listening for some little sound a hiding horse might likely make. By noon the heat had become intolerable and she had circled the meadow twice.

Back at camp she kicked out of her clothes and went to immerse herself in the river. Trout darted away, quick shadows on the white, pebbly bottom. She drank and washed the water up and across her face, through her hair.

Refreshed, she went back to camp, made a sandwich of leftover pancakes and bacon strips, and then washed down a few figs with long swigs from the canteen.

Then she dressed again to resume her search for the horse, but instead of going it on foot, she caught up Brandy, and riding bareback made wider and wider swings around the meadow.

In the end it was Brandy's anxious whinny and an answering moan which led her to a grove of pines, forward guardian stand for the forested army of pines and firs which climbed the mountain.

There on a bed of pine needles lay the little paint. In the shadows she looked like a skeleton of her old self, sunken eyes wide and frightened and orbiting in her head. Her tail was caked with dried blood, and there was foam encrusted on her nostrils. Even while Sandra, still sitting on her horse, watched, the small mare convulsed in a spasm to induce birth but nothing happened. The effort ended in a whimper which was almost human.

Sliding down from Brandy's back Sandra approached the mare. The horse was too weak to lift her ears, much less her head.

The mare's haunches were caked with filth. Blood mixed with a yellow mucus had dribbled from her vagina and was a crust where swarming flies busied themselves.

She dropped to her knees for a closer look. One tiny hoof was barely visible at the loose lips of the vagina. Then while she knelt, the mare once more went into labor and a nose and the small muzzle of a foal appeared briefly and then disappeared like a jack-in-the-box when the mare relaxed the pressure.

She knew at once the mare and the foal would never make it without help. She had been witness to literally hundreds of birthings from cat to cow, sow to mare, dog to rabbit. Most had gone off with such incredible smoothness she had stood in amazement at the utter simplicity of birth.

But then there had been others, and sometimes Gerald Deever had been called, and sometimes then a youngster had to be cut up and taken forth in pieces just to save the mother.

Sandra shuddered at the thought. The mare shuddered with her as she was wracked by another spasm, and once more the nose and part of the muzzle of the foal appeared briefly between the lips of the vagina before popping back out of sight when the pressure was off.

Sandra hadn't been able to tell by her brief glimpse of the foal if it was alive. Indeed, if the mare had been in labor as long as she thought likely, the foal might have been long beyond saving.

Getting up and turning away from the spectacle of suffering, Sandra tried to get a grip on herself, marshal her thoughts, consider the alternatives.

If she had had access to Gerald Deever's drugs, his instruments . . . but she didn't. So probably the merciful thing to do would be to ride for her rifle. Still, maybe . . . But could she?

There was one way to find out, she thought, catching up Brandy and vaulting onto her back. Digging her heels into the little horse's belly she so startled Brandy that she took off out of the pine grove like a jackrabbit with a coyote on its tail.

Scattering horses in front of her, she brought

Brandy to a hoof-gouging stop at camp. Down in a flash, she yonked the canteen from the tree limb, and then digging in the duffel came up with a bar of soap, which she shoved into the pockets of her jeans.

Back on Brandy she sent the little horse stumbling among the rocks, then racing across the meadow, and finally she reined her up with an explosive grunt in the pine grove.

First she went to the mare's muzzle, and slipping out of her shirt wet it and bathed the horse's loosely hanging lips. Then, with the dying paint following her with her eyes, she went around to where the foal was trying for an entrance into the world.

Dripping water the length of her right arm, she took the bar of soap and lathered the arm vigorously. Then she knelt, and with her left hand on the mare's haunch, delicately began to probe the vagina with her soapy hand.

Once inside the orifice, she followed the little leg until she could feel the foal's muzzle. Carefully she probed farther down along the foal's neck looking for the other leg, the leg which should have been alongside its partner at the lips of the vagina.

Then the mare convulsed, squeezed down, and her pelvic bones crushed down so tightly on Sandra's arm she couldn't contain a scream. Brandy, standing nearby, bounced into the air at the strange sound.

The spasm over, Sandra continued her blind exploration. She had seen Deever do it, not once, but many times. She had heard his running comments as he announced the nature of the trouble. But here and now that didn't seem to count for much. She didn't know what to do.

But she had to find the other leg. That much was clear. Down the neck. Back up again. Down again. Fingering carefully left and right. Searching the warm darkness. Deeper. Deeper. Finally deep as her arm would go, and then, there it was, bent way back in a crooked and impossible position that would never allow for birth, never permit the foal to clear the pelvic opening.

There was blood on her face now, and blood on her bare breasts. She was kneeling in offal, and flies hungry for the horse, for her, were crawling on her bare back.

With her fingers she explored and found the foal's knee. She must be careful now, bend just a little, an inch at a time. She moved her hand to find the tiny hoof, felt it, and ever so slowly began to bring it forward. Don't break the leg now, she told herself. Don't tear up the mare more than she is. Don't hurry.

"Pluck it carefully." She was talking softly to herself. "Tenderly. Inch by inch. Bend a little more. Bring the leg forward a little farther."

The mare convulsed again. This time Sandra stifled the scream.

"Now. Now. It's coming. Straighten it. Bring it out. Bend it a little more. Forward. Now. Straighten it."

Then there it was, the tiny hoof, next to its twin, peeking from the lips of the vagina.

Sandra sat back, but only for an instant. Grabbing the canteen she wet both arms to the elbows. She lathered them generously. Then carefully both hands went slowly back into the vagina until she had a solid but gentle hold just back of the foal's ears.

"Squeeze now, damn ya," she shouted at the mare. And when the mare obliged she pulled ever so gently.

"Squeeze again!" Encouraged by the progress or panicked by the sound of the girl's voice, the mare obliged and the foal began slipping forward and then, like a cork popping from a bottle, the tiny horse was out and lying on the pine needles.

Sandra lay back, not caring for the moment if the foal was alive or dead. All she needed now was some strength for herself. It came slowly at first in little intakes of air. Then it came in long, smooth breaths and oxygen was clearing her head, brightened her eyes, steadying her hands.

When she looked the foal was looking back at her, gasping weakly. With her hand she cleared the mucus from its muzzle. Then when it was breathing regularly she whisked it down with pine needles and dragged it around to where the mare could smell and tongue it.

Strangely, Sandra felt no exuberance. She didn't even have the strength to mount Brandy, so slipping the bridle from the horse let her go, and on foot started back toward the meadow.

Only later when she was lying in the river washing away the blood did the miracle of it hit her. It came gushing like the goodness of spring water when she heard a soft whinny, got a glimpse of a mare's head, knew the paint was on her feet.

Then the warmth of all the wonder of birth enveloped her and where the icy river water had numbed her cheeks she felt hot tears.

23

The little paint and her foal — a nearly white filly — were back in the meadow the next morning when Sandra went down to the river to bathe. Then after breakfast she walked through the tall grass for a better look.

Both mare and foal were weak, wobbly. What's more, neither seemed to be taking much nourishment — the mare because she seemed not to have an appetite for the grass, and the filly probably because there was little milk in the bony mare's udder.

At home at the ranch, this would have presented no problem. The foal would have been taken from the mare and bottle-fed until she learned how to drink from a pail, and Deever would have injected the mare with antibiotics to hasten the healing, and vitamins to restore her appetite.

But here nothing could be done. Here nature would decide the issue. One or the other, or both, might live or they might die. Watching them, Sandra felt there was hope for the mare if an infection didn't come to ravage her body. But for the filly the odds weren't good. Without milk the foal would be down again in a matter of days, or perhaps only hours.

She stood for a while watching the pair as if hoping that some miracle of recuperation might present itself. Finally she turned away and began looking for Brandy. She had decided to ride and explore road access points, and even perhaps ride the median strip through the mountain pass to find a place where she might safely drive the herd back off the road.

Brandy was on the far eastern edge of the meadow where rock and shale dropped away to desert. Rimrock was with her, and even before she got within whistling distance it was obvious that the big red stallion was paying court to the little quarter horse.

Her thoughts flew at once to Cossack. Swinging around she searched the meadow for him. When her eyes finally found him, she was relieved to see that he was so far away that he couldn't possibly see, hear, or smell what was going on down the slope.

When she turned back to look at the lovers, she felt a little thrill. Goose pimples rose on her arms as Rimrock came and threw his head over the little mare's neck.

It was such a thing as had never occurred to

her. She'd been ready to lose a horse or even several. All the while they'd marched she had felt some apprehension for the paint because she felt that even under the best circumstances the small mare might have trouble giving birth. She had anticipated that Rimrock might fight with and run off one or two mares from Cossack's harem. But the pairing off of Brandy and Rimrock had just never entered her mind.

She walked toward the pair and as far as they were concerned there were no Sandras, or any other horses, or any other creatures, not anywhere in the whole wide world. For them, there was only the red stallion and the much smaller bay mare, alone in creation's arena, driven by a force more powerful than the need to survive.

Brandy had never been bred before and she was skittish. So far as Sandra knew, neither had the stallion been at stud. Yet it was something each knew more about than finding grass, or searching out waterholes, or fighting off bears, or guiding on knee or rein or rope.

The girl was quite close when the mare finally stood still and lifted her tail to one side. With a piercing scream Rimrock was on her. Lunging forward he got her mane between his teeth, and then in a series of savage thrusts his contribution to the survival of a species was deposited in the dark, warm, and protected place where all life begins.

It was all over in seconds. Deflated, the stallion and the mare, both spraddle-legged, stood with hanging heads. Sandra was surprised to discover she was shaken by the spectacle.

She walked to the river, where she knelt and palmed the cold water up over her face. Then she drank. When she stood up again, she felt a surge of pure contentment.

Back at camp it took a strong cup of coffee to put the day back into perspective. She was going to ride, she remembered, to the road to look for access, to look for a place to hold the horses until the moment they must be pushed out onto the highway for a fast eight-mile trek over the mountain.

She had planned on riding Brandy, but now she wondered if Rimrock might not follow along. So she decided to ride the stallion.

Catching up a lead rope, she went back across the meadow. Rimrock was still standing gazing off into the distance, but Brandy was back grazing just as if nothing at all had occurred between them.

The red stallion did not move even when she walked up to him, and when she snapped the lead rope on his halter, he followed submissively in tow.

In camp she saddled him, hung the canteen on the pommel, and when she kneed him he turned obediently and walked south, out of the pasture, across the little stones, around the shelves of shale and to the edge of the desert.

24

Sandra permitted the stallion to walk for the first fifteen minutes. Then because she wanted to be back in camp before dark, she nudged him into a canter.

She followed the edge of the desert. The footing was good where the sand petered out to more substantial soil, and Rimrock, revived now, wanted to run, and so for a while she let him unlimber, shake off the lethargy, residue of his love affair.

Long before she could see the road, she heard the cars. What's more, she could see a faint haze on the desert air where fumes from exhausts marked the progress of traffic — a thin line of poison following every curve in the highway.

She walked the horse up to the road and held him while cars whizzed by. She knew she couldn't trust the stallion to put him out on the median strip between the lanes of traffic. It was difficult enough just holding him along the road where the sight of whizzing cars made his eyeballs roll.

So she turned the horse and began scouting the flatland edge for any kind of holding place, a box canyon preferably, into which she might drive the herd and control them through the night until the time was right to risk putting the horses out on the highway.

She rode a mile before she found any break in the almost monotonous terrain. It was a dry creek bed which during some springs must have carried water. She followed the dry creek bed into the foothills. It ended at a cliff which in wet times surely was a waterfall. There were high jumbles of gigantic boulders edging away from the waterfall on either side of the creek bottom. Conceivably she might hold the herd for one night between the stone walls if she were vigilant, and if the horses were well-fed and watered.

She rode farther, but there was nothing else so she urged Rimrock into his rocking-chair canter and headed for the meadow, the place she had begun to think of as home.

Long before she reached the meadow she felt an uneasiness. At first she thought the foreboding came from within herself. Then she began to realize that that wasn't the case. The horse was nervous and apprehensive. The animal, by the toss of his head, the frequent break in gait, the swerving and side-shuttling away from phantom dangers, was at the root of her own misgivings.

She tried talking to the horse, but it did no good. She pulled him back to a walk, but instead of taking a straight, smooth line, he crow-hopped and then went quartering at an angle, hard as she tried to straighten him out.

At first she thought it might be the mares. But that was ridiculous. If it had been the mares he would have run pell-mell to get back among them. Then she thought it might be an airplane she had not heard, and so she scanned the sky but there was not even a buzzard on the wing.

The closer they got to the meadow, the more rambunctious the stallion became. Finally he stopped, stood in his tracks, and when she prodded him forward he turned and went through a series of stiff-legged bucks which had her grabbing for leather.

For a moment she was tempted to cut a strong, whippy aspen branch and thrash him into submission. But she knew that would only make him wilder. In the end then, she tied him to a bush and proceeded on foot.

She went a hundred feet and turned back. There was no telling what had frightened the horse, so loosening Rimrock's saddle girth, she reached for the .30-30-caliber carbine and pulled it from the scabbard. Then she proceeded along the desert fringe and on nearing the meadow began climbing toward higher ground to where she could get a good look down on the fan-shaped stretch of greensward.

Puffing, she topped out on the shelf of shale, and wiping the sweat from her eyes, looked down on the pasture. There wasn't a horse in sight. The meadow was empty, vacated. Leaning forward she shaded her eyes for another hard look. Nothing.

Then her eyes strayed to the desert, and far out she distinguished what appeared to be a small band of three or four horses. Gradually, then, her eyes spotted other shapes which had to be horses; up among the pines, scattered among the rising shelves of shale, out on the desert . . . but not one single horse in the meadow.

She looked down at the little carbine she held. Then she levered a shell into the chamber and put the hammer at half cock. Wondering what had happened, she started down the slope and even before she came to the first fringe of grass she knew what was down there.

The message came on the breeze, stinking and unmistakable. Bear! It was a rancid, fetid odor, one which she had often smelled. One which would send any horse off on a headlong run which might take him as far as the next county.

At the first little rise in the ground she stopped. Then carefully as a hawk scans a meadow for mice, she scanned the green arena for a head, for movement in the grass, for a hulking dark form. But she saw nothing.

Likely the bear had gotten a horse. It seemed incredible that a horse would allow a bear close enough to be caught. Yet obviously it had happened. Likely he was lying somewhere in the tall grass eating it. All she could hope for was that it was a black and not a grizzly.

A black might be reluctant to leave, but could be persuaded. A grizzly? One never knew. He might retreat only to turn and come roaring back. He might charge without provocation.

The little .30-30 against a charging grizzly? A shot right between the eyes might stop him, if a gunner could aim at a galloping grizzly with such precision. Or if she could shatter a shoulder he might go down. But a bullet anywhere else, even in the heart, and he might have enough life to cover fifty or a hundred feet and knock her head off as easy as picking a blueberry.

When no swatch of swaying grass or any other sign betrayed the whereabouts of the bear, she moved cautiously forward.

In camp she found the box of rifle cartridges where she had them stashed among her extra socks and kerchiefs. She took another handful of shells and slipped them into a pocket. Then, leaning against an aspen, she stood watching and waiting.

What little wind there was came from the north straight into her face, so if there was a bear out there he would not have scented her. She wished the wind would shift, carry her smell to the bear. Sometimes that was all it took to send the animal scuttling for cover.

She stood until her left arm and left leg tingled where she had them braced against the tree. She moved, shook away the beginning of numbness in her limbs, and decided to start a

slow stalk of the meadow to see if she couldn't
startle the bear into showing himself.

It would be to her advantage to maneuver so
the wind might carry her scent to the bear.
Once he scented her, he would surely rear to
squint with his little pig eyes, rear to see what
kind of creature had come to challenge him.

Above all she didn't want to come up suddenly upon the dining carnivore. She had never
shot a bear, nor did she have any desire to do
so now. On occasion when grizzlies had drifted
down out of the foothills to menace the Bradford cattle, federal trappers had been called in.
They live-trapped the ponderous animals in
great cylindrical traps of corrugated iron and
then moved them miles back into wilderness
areas where there was no domestic stock to
harass.

So now, instead of moving straight across the
meadow, she moved along the southern fringe
toward the desert. She went like a cat, gun at
ready should the bear suddenly materialize out
of the long grass.

On reaching the barren land, she stalked
north, her eyes scanning the prairie grass, her
ears almost twitching for some small sound
which a feeding bear might make.

Though the afternoon was hardly half gone,
the sun had already slipped behind the mountains, so she hurried lest darkness come before
the confrontation.

Crossing the river in waist-deep water, she
came to the northern fringe of the meadow and
then swung west toward the mountains. Now
the breeze would carry her scent right out over

the meadow. Now, if there was a bear lying out there somewhere over the carcass of a horse, he would show himself. When that happened she would better be able to assess the situation and decide what to do.

It was difficult not to hurry. This tedious stalk had her nerves thrumming, and she would have preferred to break into a trot, scare the bear, get it over with.

But she bit her lower lip and forced herself to maintain a slow, steady pace, a cautious stalk. Many times she paused, surveyed the meadow intently, listened for the crack of a bone between giant jaws, a slurping of a greedy animal sucking at internal juices, a low warning rumble . . . but there was nothing.

Here, on the north side of the meadow with the wind blowing away from her, the odor of the bear was less discernible. Perhaps the bear had only come, and then not being able to run down a horse, fled back into its foothill home country.

Likely that was it, she decided as she came almost to the end of the meadow's northern boundary line. A bear's odor was sometimes so strong it lingered for hours. Several times in the past she had come upon stumps torn up by a bear conducting an ant, an insect search, and though she could tell by all the signs that the bear had left hours before, the strong smell lingered on.

Approaching the fringe of pines, the grove in which she had given the paint mare a birthing assist, she stopped, lowered her gun from ready, and with a deep sigh of relief was about to conclude that the bear had gone.

The letdown was a debilitating experience. Suddenly she felt her muscles, her tendons, her bones, her spirit melt like the tallow of a candle in the last hot liquid of its bright life. In a word, she was drained.

And then it was, while standing there with every defense at rest, that the warning growl came out of the dusky grove in which the paint mare had foaled.

Had she been alert she would have instantly and instinctively raised her gun for whatever action was necessary. As it was, she stood numbed, hardly believing that the bear was there in the gloom cast by the thick pines, maybe less than a hundred feet from where she stood.

It took another warning rumble to unfreeze her. She realized retreat was already impossible, that her only defense was to attack.

Then she held the rifle high so as not to hit the bear. Unwilling to risk the rage of a wounded animal, she cocked the gun and shot. In quick succession she levered shells and shot two more times into the tops of the pines, leaving two shells in case the bear charged.

Then she listened, heard brush crackle and rocks roll as the animal fled. Quickly she jammed more shells into the little rifle, and then prepared herself for the long wait.

Shifting from leg to leg, unlimbering her arms from time to time, fanning away at the flies, working up saliva for her dry mouth, and peering, peering into the gloomy stand of pine she waited half an hour. It seemed like an eternity.

Then slowly she went forward. Finally her eyes adjusted to the gloom beneath the thick pines. She saw the remains of the foal which only yesterday she had helped into the world, and the grisly sight turned her stomach, sent shivers up her arms.

Scouting the grove for tracks she found one at the edge of a pine grove in the dusting hollow left by a fool hen. It was an enormous track, undoubtedly that of a grizzly. Once more she felt the goose pimples run the length of her arm, felt the tendons tighten in her neck.

That the grizzly would be back she never doubted. Perhaps already he was stalking her, getting ready to return to claim his kill, haul away what hadn't been eaten to cache for some future time.

Once more she went over to look at what was left of the tiny foal. More than half of the animal had been eaten. But there were no tears. There was nothing left to cry for.

Slowly she backed out of the pine grove. When she was clear of it, she turned her back on the trees and crossed the meadow to her camp. Leaving her gun she went to where Rimrock was tethered. When he wouldn't be led, she took off his saddle and bridle and turned him loose. Then bent under the weight of the saddle she was carrying, she went back to camp.

Though she was almost certain the bear had

no designs on her, she gathered extra firewood. Then she got out the map and wrote:

"Eleventh night. July 8. Grizzly killed the paint's foal. What next?"

Each time on awakening during the night, she added fuel to the fire. Then the night of startling dreams was suddenly over, the sun was coming up out of the desert, and there, standing looking down at her was Dr. Paul Pelham, eyes bright and snapping, an impish grin separating the bright white hairs of his whiskers. Looking over his shoulder was Bessie.

25

"I heard shots," Dr. Pelham said, by way of greeting.

Trying to smooth her tangle of black hair, Sandra got up on an elbow and said, "Bear."

"Get him?"

"I didn't try. Shot over his head."

"Grizzly?"

Sandra nodded.

"Did he get a horse?"

"A foal. Two days old."

"I was worried," Dr. Pelham said.

"You needn't have been," Sandra lied.

The doctor took Bessie's lead rope and walked off toward a neighboring grove of aspens. "I'll take a walk while you get up."

After a breakfast of bacon and flapjacks Sandra checked her rifle and she and the man moved across the meadow to the pine grove where the grizzly had dined.

"Gone," Sandra said, looking down at the blood spots where the filly carcass had lain.

"He came back to get it and cache it," Dr. Pelham said.

"Think he'll leave it at that?" Sandra asked.

"No. He'll be back. It was too easy. He won't forget."

"That's what I figured. Well, I'll be gone."

"When do you figure on leaving?"

"Tomorrow, if all the horses come back."

They both turned. Most of the horses were back in the meadow. A few were still along the perimeter, but if they wanted grass there was no other place to go.

Sandra scraped pine needles and tried to cover the bloodstains. "I'm sorry I bothered you," she said. "I had no idea the sound of a rifle would carry that far."

"No bother. In this clear mountain air sound carries great distances. And anyway, I was afraid for you, and then too it gave me an excuse which I welcomed. The excuse to visit you."

"Thank you."

"No thanks. Lately the solitary life has lost its original mystical attraction. Not even the brandy is working the miracles that it formerly did. As I grow older, I feel more and more the need of people. I even think in my old age I might just become a garrulous and probably pesty old man."

"Never. Not you."

They started out of the pine grove back across the meadow.

"If you leave tomorrow," Dr. Pelham asked, "when will you put the horses on the road?"

"Three o'clock the next morning. With luck maybe I can have them over the mountain and back off the road by six — in three hours."

"Are you afraid?"

"Yes."

"Don't be. You've gotten this far and lost but two foals. You'll make it."

"I wish I had your confidence."

"You do," Dr. Pelham smiled.

"I surely don't feel it."

"But you do. It's there. If you didn't have it you'd never have started out in the first place. Then you'd have quit, turned back when the airplane came, or when the desert became unbearable. You've got confidence. You just don't recognize it."

"It's nice to hear you say it."

Halfway across the meadow Sandra turned to say, "You going right back this morning?"

"No, I'm going on into Sago."

"But you were just there."

"I know, but would you believe I forgot to call my secretary to see if there were any messages which might need my attention."

"You forgot?" Sandra gave the professor an inquiring, almost suspicious look.

"No. Not really. I think I just like going to Sago. You see, in an old hotel there's an old saloon with a mahogany bar and big brass spittoons. It's restful as the mountains."

Sandra laughed. "And I'll bet it's in the basement, and I'll bet it is shadowy, almost dark and it is cool in that old saloon. And I'll bet you have some interesting people to talk to."

"How did you know?"

"Well, my father likes to go to just such a place in Three Bends. It's the kind of place I'd expect you to look for too."

Now it was Dr. Pelham's turn to laugh. "You've got my number, haven't you?"

Sandra smiled and looked away.

In camp the doctor picked up Bessie's lead line and headed for the desert fringe.

"Watch out for that bear," he said, turning to wave good-bye.

26

Sandra carried the rifle all that day. She did not anticipate that the bear would be back so long as he still had not finished eating the cached filly, but nobody, not even the best of the country's mammalogists, could predict what a grizzly might do.

During the morning she made a head count of the horses. Then, saddling Brandy, she made a test roundup to see what difficulties might be anticipated when tomorrow's drive began.

It was almost too easy. The horses, well fed and fattening now, had come to accept her presence on the back of the little cutting horse, and she had no trouble bringing them together.

Within an hour of easy riding she had every animal concentrated into a milling circle of slowly moving horses directly in the middle of the pasture.

All horses, that is, except Rimrock. But about him there was no worry. Where the mares went he would follow.

She spent the afternoon bathing and washing her clothes and discarding what gear she figured she could do without. At least half of her foodstuff would be left behind. Brandy would be given one half of the remaining oats in the evening, and the other half in the morning. Her saucepan went because she would have nothing to cook. An ounce here and an ounce there, until she had little left other than her rainproof poncho, her bedroll and, of course, the rifle.

Getting the horses to the road and then over the concrete pass which cut through the mountains would be Brandy's job. Any extra weight would make that job just that much more difficult.

Especially during the road trek, Brandy would have to be her eyes, her ears, her instincts. She would have to depend on the little horse to let no animal of the herd stray or filter back behind them. She would have to trust the little horse completely. Even in bright moonlight one or another or even a knot of horses might break away, head back for the grass and water in the meadow.

She especially dreaded a whole nighttime of holding them beneath the dry waterfall among the disarray of huge boulders. If there had been water, it would have been easier. By then the horses would be hungry and thirsty. They'd all have visions of the lush meadow they had only just left, visions of the clear stream of cold water, and all of them would feel the need to return.

Finished eating, she got out the map and wrote:

"Twelfth night. July 9. Tomorrow the big push."

So she slept poorly and was awake even before the moon was down and the sun was ready to accept its responsibilities for the day. Though she wasn't hungry, she made herself eat a big breakfast because it might be her last real meal for a long time.

Then, making sure the last ember of her breakfast fire was cold, she went out into the tall dry grass to catch up Brandy. While she was saddling her, the mare ate the remaining portion of oats with drooling delight.

Swinging about she looked around to see if among the things she was abandoning there was not some item she might wish later she had taken. Then she mounted and, guiding Brandy at a slow walk, she began circling the meadow. It was like pulling an invisible cord around the scattered horses until once again she had a loose knot of animals milling lazily about in the middle of the grassy area.

She gave Brandy the direction, and the drive began. All went well until the herd reached the edge of the meadow. Then the rebellion broke out. Horses began breaking away in knots, to return to the grass. Letting Brandy have her head, Sandra and the horse sent the mavericks galloping back.

It was a grinding, sweating, jarring half hour before Grandma, the lead mare, gave up and began the southern trek along the sandy desert fringe. The rest of the herd fell in behind her. Then Cossack began a rearguard action nipping reluctant mares to keep the line moving.

From time to time one or another of the herd decided to turn back. But Brandy anticipated these rebellious ones and was out there with the swiftness of a well-trained sheep dog to turn them back into the line of march.

Then the southward trek turned into tedium. It became a seemingly endless trek and there was always the heat of the sun blinding on the white rocks, lying like fire on the saddle leather.

Toward noon Sandra directed Brandy to turn them higher into the foothills into the shade of a butte. She felt the need to unlimber her legs. The horses stood, heads hanging, while Sandra dismounted and ate a few dates which had begun to ferment in her shirt pocket. Then she took a long, refreshing drink from her canteen, and wished she could offer it to members of the herd.

In half an hour she was mounted again, and with Brandy gently nudging the group here and there got them started again.

In the midday heat the pace slowed perceptibly, and the last horse in the long line was the little paint mare who had lost her filly to the grizzly.

On and on they went. The monotony of Brandy's unshod hooves making soothing, rhythmical sounds in the sand had Sandra half hypnotized, just beyond the edge of sleep. Sometimes she would come awake with a start, and swaying in the saddle wondered where she was.

Sleeping in the saddle was no trick for her. If she had been alone, she would have allowed herself to doze, knowing Brandy would not only keep her out of trouble, but travel a straight line.

But now she made herself stay awake. There was no telling when the lead mare would have her bellyful of the tedious trek and decide to return to the grassy meadow and the cold river. And once the mare turned, the herd would follow. It would take a lot of hard riding, perhaps more than the little mare could take in this heat, to turn the stampede and once again get the herd headed toward the road.

Yet despite her efforts to stay awake, Sandra dozed. And in her torpid mind she kept hearing an airplane engine, and then jerking herself awake she would listen, but then there would be nothing except the shuffling of horses' unshod hooves in the sand, the snuffling and snorting, the creaking of the saddle leather and sometimes the jingle of bridle rings as Brandy made an adjustment to the bit between her teeth.

Then her mind, asking to make up for the sleep she had lost the night before, would retreat again and then, as before, she could hear the muffled roar of an approaching plane.

Suddenly it was real. The memory of other planes jogged the horses into a trot. Sandra wheeled Brandy to the desert side of the herd to turn them into the brushy foothills. Then she looked up and saw it was the same plane looping the loop, diving on a dead engine, roaring back into life to climb and do a wing over.

She rode hard to keep the herd from breaking apart. She wondered why the airplane had returned. The herd could never be driven back across the desert without killing every last animal. There was no railroad in the vicinity for loading.

The plane dived straight at her. The nose of the craft lifted and as it passed over she saw a tiny white object blossom into a tiny parachute and fall to the ground.

The plane gave the same sardonic wing waggle it had insulted her with before, and in seconds was only a silver glint far out across the desert on its way back to Three Bends.

She waited until the horses had resumed walking before going back. The parachute was a plain white handherchief with strings from its four corners to a small rock. Wrapped around the rock was a piece of paper.

She unfolded the paper and read: "This is the end of the line. In three weeks every last horse will be back on our side of the desert."

27

The full significance of the note would not become clear to her until later. As she folded the paper and put it into her shirt pocket along with the remaining fermented dates, she wondered if the wild horse killers had concocted some new scheme to stop her.

But what? Shoot the horses along the roadside and truck the carcasses to the Three Bends freezers? Couldn't be. They'd all be jailed.

She stopped the horse, brought out the note, and read it again: "This is the end of the line. In three weeks every last horse will be back on our side of the desert."

Perhaps they had concluded that she'd never be able to manage a mountain crossing. But that would have been pure speculation on their part.

They were right in part. If she didn't get the horses through the mountain pass they would eventually drift back to their home range. Even the lush meadow wasn't big enough to hold a herd that size, not once the grass began to wither, to die.

She looked out over the line of march. The horses were beginning to string out. She had to take the kinks out of the line, to bunch them up. Kneeing Brandy, she began slowly to close the formation, weld it into a more manageable unit.

Already she could see the fumes which faintly outlined the progress of traffic along the road. The sun, long gone behind the mountains, would sink soon into the faraway sea. Then there would be a couple of hours of almost complete darkness before the moon came thrusting up out of the desert.

The dry creek bed, with its clutter of fist-sized stones, appeared through an opening in the brush. She leaned forward, signaling Brandy to break into a canter.

Expertly the cutting horse turned the herd, headed them up the incline.

They were tired and thirsty and easy to herd. As if benumbed, they took the line of least resistance, responding to a galloping horse with a girl twirling a rope end.

Grandma, the lead mare, stayed to the middle of the dry creek bed. It was the easiest route since boulders and brush lined the banks. When she came to the face of the dry waterfall Grandma stopped and turned to look back inquiringly.

Brandy eased off, slowed, and then gradually

the stragglers caught up with the hammer-headed mare. The herd stood bunched, glad not to have to move farther, content for the moment at least to rest first one and then another leg, and take the strain off their necks by letting their heads hang.

Sandra slipped out of the saddle and fastening Brandy to a bankside bush, searched her saddle pack for a loaf of brick-hard bread. Breaking off a chunk, she swilled water to wash down the mouthfuls of crust.

Then standing off from her horse in the middle of the dry creek bed where she could get a better look at the physical characteristics and arrangement of her dead-end corral, she tried to anticipate what subsequent moves the herd might make once they'd revived.

That they would revive was certain. Soon as the blistering rocks around had cooled, soon as darkness crept up out of the desert, they would come out of their lethargy and typically begin a hunt for water.

If they moved straight down the creek bed, stopping them would be easy. And that would be their first move. After that they would seek other avenues of escape, and Sandra now saw there were many.

As she saw it she had only one advantage. They could not move anywhere as a herd, unless they took the creek bed route. The other avenues of escape were narrow, twisting aisles between brush and boulders wide enough to accommodate one horse, or perhaps two or three horses at the most. This removed the danger of a stampede.

She hoped, with the help of Brandy, she might be able to turn back the more ambitious of the lot, until at last tiring, they might be willing to wait the night out.

Yet, hard as she would like to have believed it, she knew the horses would not content themselves with just waiting. Soon as the night cooled they would have visions of the icy river coursing through the green meadow, and they would try again and again throughout the night to slip away, hit the desert edge, and head back for the green oasis.

Walking back to Brandy she loosened her saddle girth and wished there was yet another measure of oats to feed her. Then taking down the canteen, she went to the horse's head and pouring a few swallows into her hat for the horse, she proffered it. Long after the water had been gulped down, the horse continued to tongue the wet hat.

"That's all, girl. That's all," she said, putting her hat back on.

When darkness came she tightened the saddle girth, mounted, and took a position in the exact center of the creek bed.

Up to then the horses had not moved except to flap their heads at flies, switch their tails, shift from leg to leg, or scratch, one against the other, or against any convenient rock outcropping.

The first bid for freedom came about a half hour after darkness. Even before she heard the hoof sounds of approaching horses, she felt the quarter horse tense beneath her.

"Easy, Brandy," Sandra said gently. With

reins slack then, Sandra permitted Brandy to move forward and turn the dim shadows of horses back.

After that she could hear the restlessness. Pawing hooves. Snuffling and shaking, and then a piercing neigh — without a doubt Cossack — followed by a chorus of lesser whinnies.

Sandra felt Brandy lean forward, and knew once more they were starting down the creek bed. The cutting horse moved, but this time the herd chose to ignore her, and when the profile of the hammerhead mare came into clear view, Sandra swung a rope until it whistled, and shouted, "Hey ya! Hey ya!"

The whistling rope turned them, and she heard the clatter of stones as they retreated to the face of the dry waterfall.

The moon! Where was the moon? The promise of it was there, a soft glow along the eastern horizon. But why didn't it show its face?

Brandy must have sensed Sandra's concern. Instead of waiting, she patrolled from left to right, across the small stones of the dry creek bed.

"Easy, Brandy. Easy." Sandra tried to quiet the horse.

Meanwhile the herd had quieted. Sandra did not like it. Sitting there straining her eyes in the dark, she wondered what they were up to. She didn't have to wait long. With a jerk that almost sent her backward out of the saddle, Brandy was off and into the brush.

Sandra threw up an arm to protect her face, and grabbing the saddle pommel, let the cutting horse have her way.

When Brandy came to an abrupt halt, she got a glimpse of a white horse turning, and then she heard him breaking branches as he battered his way back to the herd. Cossack, she thought. He had tried to sneak away among the boulders, through the brush.

By the time she got back to the dry creek bed, the moon was up. First she saw the gleaming white eye of Spook, the walleyed horse. Then she began to recognize other contours: the high head of Rimrock, the hammerhead of Grandma, the slight form of the little paint who had lost her filly, the bony outlines of Knuckles, the awkward shuffle of Stumbles . . .

But if the moon with its welcoming white glow made it easier for Sandra to keep tabs on the horses, it also encouraged them to bolder tactics.

Instead of breaking away singly, two, three, and even four would suddenly angle off. No sooner would Brandy turn these back than there would be other deserters to contend with.

Thorns slashed her skin and whippy branches left welts as Sandra rode back and forth, in and out, often at full gallop. With Brandy sometimes treading timidly on loose shale, sometimes leaping rocks and bounding over brush, it turned into a nightmare of chasing ghosts, of horses streaking back and forth — whinnying with fright, with thirst, with hunger.

Only the rough terrain kept the herd from forming up for a stampede. Bewildered, some escaped, only to return because herd instinct kept them from galloping alone the long miles back to water.

But some did not come back. Banding together, they waited out on the smoother desert terrain for the others to join them. Only when Brandy went to her knees, and Sandra went over her head to come to a bruising halt against a boulder, did she admit to herself that her plan had failed, that the horses could not be contained massed beneath the dry waterfall.

Retrieving her hat, she caught up a trembling Brandy, but instead of mounting, she led her down the creek bed out onto the desert.

Here, away from the shadows of cliffs and rocks and bushes, the moon made the night almost bright as day. All around her, confused horses wandered, waiting for a leader, waiting to be reunited in a herd before making the long journey back to water.

Sandra seized the opportunity. Leaping aboard Brandy she began gently to nudge remaining horses into a tightly milling herd a hundred yards out beyond the edge of the foothill cover.

Then she rode circle on them, listening to the anxious whinnies of horses still lost and bewildered. Horses in the milling herd answered, and then here, there, and from many places, confused horses stepped out into the moonlight and trotted swiftly, glad to be reunited with the others.

After that, to Sandra's surprise, it became easier. Brandy settled down immediately once free of the hazardous terrain, and with a minimum of effort kept strays filtering back into the clot of horses. Then when no more horses seemed left in the brush, Sandra tried for a head count. She couldn't be sure, but she thought all had been accounted for.

Only Rimrock refused to join the herd. There was the threat of Cossack, but it was something else too. Perhaps he realized that he didn't really belong. Maybe such individuality as comes from being raised as one person's property had robbed him of some of his herd instinct. Anyway, he paced the perimeter, inquiring regularly about any mares who might be agreeable to a tryst.

But no mares answered him. Gradually the herd quieted, ceased its perpetual milling, and settling themselves in head-hanging postures of repose, and alternating resting legs, slept.

Sandra slept too, sometimes, slumped in the saddle, while Brandy kept watch. The moon climbed the sky and started down toward the mountains, and coyotes sometimes threaded the night stillness with their sharp needles of sound, and pygmy desert owls sailed over, and once, high on the mountainside, a puma caterwauled.

At midnight Sandra, feeling rested, started mentally to brace herself for that crucial part of the trek which all along she had most feared.

She could face the desert or even the airplane. But an unsuspecting public, hurtling their autos through the morning darkness to be confronted suddenly by an undisciplined herd of half-ton wild horses . . .

Was the road going to be her Waterloo? Did she have the right to go on the highway and perhaps endanger human life? Was this the one really weak link, the one indefensible act in what she felt certain was an otherwise morally justifiable venture?

She wondered, and the minutes ticked away, and the moon hurried toward the mountain peaks, and then it was time, time to jar the herd awake, time to start them toward the highway.

Part Four

28

Long before she got to the highway she could see car headlights blinking like fireflies as they flashed through the breaks in the roadside trees.

It was incredible, the number of autos on the four lanes of the roadway going east and west. She had expected the highway to be all but deserted, that traffic at three o'clock in the morning would have dwindled to the intermittent vehicle.

The closer she came, the more convinced she became that to put a band of thirty wild horses out among those speeding cars would result in nothing less than a carnage — a tangle of wrecked automobiles and dead and dying humans and horses.

Where was everybody going, and at that time of the morning? Then it occurred to her. She was seeing men going to the mines which were scattered throughout the area, seeing moonlighting ranchers commuting to work. It was, of course, because of the recession and some ranchers she knew commuted as far as a hundred miles just to hold jobs while wife and children tended the small spreads they had set off back somewhere away from the main roads.

She thought of the note in her shirt pocket: "This is the end of the line."

It *was* the end of the line. She knew it now. To have to turn back, recross the desert, and turn the herd loose on the prairie where the plane would be waiting . . . to come straggling home . . . beaten . . . Her heart actually seemed to stop beating and there was a numbness in her fingers and the breeze down from the mountains felt icy on her cheeks.

To have come all this way, to have tortured the horses and herself . . . for nothing.

Even as the herd continued to plod toward the highway, even while the swoosh and whine and roar of traffic was becoming louder in her ears, she could see it would eventually end with a long line of glassy-eyed horses staggering into the loading pens at Three Bends. She could see the magnificent Cossack broken, his pink nostrils caked with black, dried blood; see the watch horse, her white eyes red from running; see Grandma, her hooves dragging in the sand, blood dripping from her mouth. The little paint? The one who had lost her foal to the grizzly?

She'd never make it, but probably would ride into Three Bends across the back seat of a jeep, a bullet hole in her head.

She could see the men gathering around the jeep to drink beer and celebrate, while the wild herd stood like cardboard figures of crippled horses, muzzles touching the acrid earth churned to dust by the thousands who in turn had come to be converted from livestock into deadstock.

She was almost to the highway before she regained her composure enough to knee Brandy out, around, and past the herd so she could turn them back.

Gradually, when the lead mare stopped, the herd closed in and bunched up around her. Then she guided Grandma back, weaving her way through the mass of horses to strike out once more down the long trail she had just traversed.

When they had all been turned around, and Grandma was about to start moving toward the faraway oasis of green grass and cold water, something made Sandra pull Brandy up to a sharp and jolting halt. What had happened? Something was different. What was it? What had changed? What suddenly was missing?

She looked over the herd, all sharply visible in the moonlight, and she could see nothing amiss. She listened, but the night sounds were comparable to night sounds of any other night. Then suddenly and stunningly she realized that she heard no autos. Swinging her little horse around, she rose in the stirrups. There wasn't a car headlight in sight.

For a moment she was too surprised to do

anything but stand there in the stirrups waiting for the traffic to resume its roar. When it didn't, she sent Brandy galloping toward a break in the trees. Pushing through, she rode out onto the shoulder of the road, surprised to see a short distance to the east two big semi-trailer trucks jackknifed at such an angle that they completely blocked the highway.

She walked Brandy toward the trucks, assuming there had been an accident, and just as the horse's hooves hit the concrete and began to clip-clop, a man darted out from the shadows and came running toward her.

When he came alongside he asked in a loud whisper, "You've got the horses?"

She was too surprised to answer. She swallowed hard and nodded her head vigorously.

"Well, for God's sake get them out on the road and get going. Traffic is already beginning to pile up behind us. The cops will be here any minute."

There was no time to ask herself how this thing could be. There was only time to act, and she put Brandy recklessly down the road embankment, whipped her with a rope end so she went bolting through the roadside border of trees, and came down on the herd at a dead gallop.

Getting out in front, she rode right up alongside Grandma and with a cut on the neck from the rope, turned her. Then pushing Brandy as she never had before, she struck out here and there, hitting any horse within reach, until she had the herd heading pell-mell for the opening in the trees.

And Brandy stretched herself. Tired as she must have been, she ran close to the ground with such bursts of speed that when the wild ones hit the trees branches broke with a resounding crash.

Out on the glistening moonlit highway Sandra maneuvered east to turn the herd west. The horses had scattered. Some were running the east concourse and some the west one, except all were headed in a westerly direction. Gradually, all except one or another a bit more boneheaded than the rest settled for the soft, grassy median strip.

Only then did Sandra take time for a backward glance. It seemed a hundred headlights had already been stacked in a long double line behind the stalled trucks. Even above the thudding of hooves she could hear impatient car horns and now and again an impatient shout. She knew that if a state patrol car hadn't already arrived, it wouldn't be more than a matter of minutes before one would.

But her job was to drive the horses, and she meant to. Tired, hungry, thirsty . . . it didn't matter now. They were going to run, and Brandy and she would see to it.

It was a raceway. In cutting through the mountain the road builders had left insurmountable rock precipices on either side of the wide highway. Here no horse could shunt off, take his own direction. Here it was straight ahead or turn back to get a taste of the stinging rope she held at the ready.

But none of the horses were turning back. What had started out as a drive now turned into a stampede. They were going full out right down the middle of the median. Sandra rode so close to the last horse in the herd, she could hear her grunt every time her hooves hit the ground.

The horses could not maintain the stampede pace. Gradually as the incline became steeper, they began to slow down. Sandra had a chance for another look back. There must have been a mile of headlights backed up behind the trucks. She could see red lights flashing. The highway patrol had arrived.

By the time they reached the summit of the pass, the horses would all have been more than glad just to walk, but with rope swinging and her voice shrilling out with "Hey ya! Get on! Get on!" she kept them trotting.

When they broke over the summit there far below in the east lane was yet another long line of car headlights with red lights flashing here and there up front of the immobilized column. Obviously there was also an obstruction in the east lane, and likely, Sandra reasoned, two more huge semi-trailer trucks were jack-knifed across the highway there.

Going downhill the horses picked up a little speed. Sandra, realizing that at any moment the state police might clear the roadway, permitting an avalanche of autos to hurtle down all four highway lanes, kept pressure on the herd, kept them going as fast as she felt she could without running them to death.

As they galloped down the west slope, closer and closer to the long line of headlights in the east lane, Sandra began to scan the sheer walls of solid rock, looking for a break through which she might get the herd off into the backcountry.

She also kept an eye cocked to the rear for the horde of angry motorists that would at any moment come surging across the summit.

Down and down the herd traveled, lower and lower, until she could hear the horns honking, hear a siren, see shadows moving past the headlights. Down and down until she was out of the mountains and the road was beginning to level off.

Then suddenly a bright light appeared in front of the trotting horses, breaking the herd into two segments. She rode right on through, and there holding a flashlight stood a grinning Dr. Pelham, his eyes twinkling in the moonlight, his white beard parted and his teeth shining white in a mischievous grin.

"In here," he said, swinging the light to point to a roadside sign which read REST AREA.

"Dr. Pelham!" Sandra gasped.

"Get them in here. There's a hikers' trail beyond, going off into the woods." The impish smile disappeared. "Now!" he said in a tone of command.

She swung Brandy, got out ahead of Hammerhead, and turned her. Then whipping Brandy left and right, back and forth, making her rope whistle and her voice sound out with a "Hey ya!" she brought the herd to the turnoff which led into the rest area.

When the last horse was off the highway she turned. Dr. Pelham waved, blew her a kiss, and turning started down toward the throngs of furious motorists and the police.

The horses walked now. Between the picnic tables. Among the garbage cans. Past the rest rooms, out onto the hiking trail.

As the last horse disappeared down the trail, Sandra turned in time to see the headlights of the autos begin to surge up the mountain pass. She could see the lights of a police helicopter above the moving autos, hear the throb of its engine.

And then she remembered Dr. Pelham's words: ". . . we gain as many friends by accepting favors as by giving them . . ." And now she was ready to believe it.

29

The exhausted herd, hassled to the limits of their endurance, showed no inclination to leave the path hikers had forged through the forest, and were content to walk single file, muzzle to flank, with their usually twitching tails hanging as limply as their lowered heads.

Morning came gradually on the west side of the mountain. Accustomed to having day break abruptly, bright with the sun suddenly popping over the desert horizon, Sandra had the strange feeling of having suddenly come into an alien land.

But alien feelings aside, more important, there was no grass. And even worse, there was no water.

Mostly now the horses moved like mechanical toys. Gone was the wild exhilaration. It was true what they said about the wild mustang: They had hearts as strong as the flint they sent flaking and flying beneath their pounding hooves. But it was also true that they were made of such flesh and bone and blood as finally must succumb, wilt the wild spirit.

It was full light now. Sandra supposed it would be several hours yet before the searing sun topped the mountains and she was glad for the cool shadows, for the breeze which came up from the valley which the trees shrouded from view.

Somehow she had to get a look into that valley, survey this last obstacle between the horses and safety, the Rantan Reservation.

But first they all had to have water. Then they had to have food. And there was neither here in this niggardly forest.

So she followed along, the last in the long line of weary animals plodding north because to the south was the highway with its nightmare of cars, to the east rose the mountain peaks and to the west somewhere down there in the valley were thousands of endless acres of grapes, and men to keep a maverick horse herd from wreaking havoc.

Sometimes Sandra's head nodded on her shoulders, and she slept briefly only to come awake with such a violent wrench of her head that her neck muscles felt as if they'd been jerked from their moorings.

And the roof of tall pines sighed monotonously, and the floor of soft needles muffled the sound of horses' hooves, and the march became an endless succession of scaly tree trunks identical as railroad ties, one looking just like every other one — endlessly along the side of the mountain.

The hikers' path narrowed until it was a faint trail, but still the horses followed it. And Sandra's mind began to play tricks with her.

In such a state of bewildered exhaustion Sandra never noticed a quickening of pace, a deliberate outstepping of horses that brought the line of marchers to a slow trot. Stinging branches of trees across her face revived her. She was certain at once that the herd had smelled water. The strongest horses barged ahead, pushing the weaker ones off the dim trail. She had to hold Brandy in for her own and the horses' safety, because the tough little quarter horse was all for going out around the herd, through the punishing reach of whipping branches.

By the time the herd broke into the clearing most of the horses were galloping. Sandra saw at once that it was a wide burn, perhaps a thousand acres where fire had come not too many years ago, and where now charred stumps still stood like blackened tombstones to the dead trees of yesterday.

At the edge of the burn Sandra reined Brandy to a halt. But the rest of the herd went straight to the middle of the big burn and at once there were anxious neighs, whinnies of pain, shrill screams of excited horses where they had gathered for what was obviously a biting, kicking free-for-all.

She rode over to break it up. But this time the whistling rope, her shouts of "Hey ya! Hey ya!" were ignored. She dismounted and found a whip strong enough to put a knob on even the hardest head.

Back on her horse and wielding the club, she scattered horses so she could come to the center of the melee, and then she saw what all the excitement was about. From beneath a rock a pitifully slender trickle of water flowed to form a sump of mud where an old tree trunk must have once stood.

The horses were fighting one another for the water, trampling the sump into a mass of mud. With the club to hold off any brave enough to challenge her, she dismounted again and jumped into the mudhole. Seeing her on the ground was enough. The horses backed off. Dropping to her knees she began to clean out the mudhole with her bare hands. The horses, encircling her, licked at the globs of mud she tossed up, and as one or another became brave enough to come close, she reached for the club and sometimes she landed a blow and a horse retreated squealing.

From whence came this last surge of strength she could not guess. But suddenly she was no longer tired. When the ends of her fingers began to turn raw, she got up from her knees, and going to a charred pine stump, gave it a kick; it shattered into splendidly flat and shovel-like slabs.

Back in the hole with a slab of pine, she sent the mud flying until she came to the minerals the mountains were made of. Then she enlarged the hole until it was as wide as she was tall. She crawled on her hands and knees to where the water was trickling from beneath the rock and with a stick began probing until she had augered a large hole and the water from beneath the rock tripled in volume.

Below, the basin she had dug began to fill. Now that the mud had been removed the water was clear. She knelt to drink, and though it smacked slightly of sulfur, it was potable. Now all she had to do was to keep the horses from once more trampling it into a morass.

Well, let the bravest come first, she thought, and she backed off just a little way and Grandma and Cossack moved forward. Without ever taking their eyes from her, they drank, and when she thought they had had enough, she swung the club, and they backed off and Rimrock and Knuckles took a turn. Then came Spook and a big bay she had never gotten around to naming. And it amazed her that there was a minimum of shoving, of biting and kicking, except the whinnying of those at the outer perimeter was so loud she wanted to clap her hand over her ears to keep the sound out.

But finally the last ones came, and then all alone the little paint mare who had lost her foal came to the watering hole. Then Sandra led Brandy over and the horse lowered her head and the water bulged in her throat as it went down in great gulps.

When the last had drunk the first were back for more. And the trickle from beneath the rock was surprisingly ample, and if the basin collapsed in some places, muddying the water, it didn't stop the horses.

Though it seemed to have taken an endless amount of time, the whole herd had watered within less than two hours. Already they were fanning out, searching for the meager tufts of grass, browsing on the buds, leaves, and tender branch ends of the deciduous trees which were sprouting to take the place of the pines which had burned.

It was no place to hold a horse herd, Sandra knew, but it would have to do because there would be no meadows on the mountainside. And below, in the valley, were the grapes.

And now that she could turn her attention to the valley, she could see that there were more grapes. There were fields of lettuce, and acres of celery, but mostly as far as an eye could reach either north or south it was vineyards, tidy row on row of grapevines stretching right up to the hovering mountains.

They were trapped in a pocket. She could see no way from her vantage point through or around the fertile valley. To the north the mountain range circled west to cut her off. To the south was the highway and more mountains, and below, the grapes.

The horses might be content to stay in the burn for two, or even perhaps three days. But then they would begin to gravitate to the valley as surely as water runs downhill, and in the end, no matter what measures she took, the horses would get to the valley and then the trouble would start.

But she was too tired to think. After unburdening Brandy of the saddle, she made a pillow of it just above the sump hole. Then before lying down she got out the map and wrote:

"Fourteenth morning. July 11. Over the mountain. God bless Dr. Pelham."

Then she put her head back on the saddle and in seconds was sound asleep.

The pulsing of a helicopter engine awakened her. The awkward, silly-looking, silver copter, flopping along like some prehistoric monster, came over low enough to scatter the horses.

Looking up she saw the pilot wave, and from an open door a camera with a long lens was methodically making a celluloid record of her presence in the big burn with the band of wild horses.

Then, just as she began to fear the copter might scatter the herd beyond her capability of regrouping it, the machine slid off and away in an abrupt maneuver and disappeared behind the crests of the trees which surrounded the burn like a living green wall.

It was obvious these were not horse killers. More likely it was a police machine adding the last damning evidence to Dr. Pelham's ingenious maneuver at disrupting all traffic on one of the nation's major transcontinental highways.

The thought of the troubles Dr. Pelham might face made further sleep impossible. Instead she went to the tiny waterhole, cleaned out the mud again, and shored up the banks with charred branches of the old forest.

Then she went back to the saddle and found a can of beans, a bar of chocolate, the heel of a loaf of bread, and settled down to dine.

If nothing else, she thought as she ate, I've lost at least two inches around the waist. Her belt was in the last hole, and it hung loosely around her middle. One way to diet, she thought wryly, as she wolfed down the beans and then nibbled the chocolate slowly to make the sweet taste last longer.

Supper finished, she went to the waterhole and filled her canteen. Then she went back to sit with her head against the saddle. The herd was pretty much scattered across the burn, but the tempo of feeding had slacked off, and she could see that some of the stronger horses were getting the pecking order back in operation by running lesser citizens of their social order away from more desirable grazing tracts.

Rimrock and Cossack were giving one another the evil eye again. Between them was a mare who, if Sandra guessed correctly, would tonight or tomorrow be inviting one or the other over for a rather consequential tête-à-tête.

But that is the way it was, she philosophized. Life went on come whatever hell or high water. Well, let them have at it, she thought, but now I want to sleep. She had hardly closed her eyes when several of the herd nickered and brought her abruptly awake.

She sat up instantly alert. Every horse, wherever he was, stood with head high, ears alert, looking in the same direction.

She looked too. A rider materialized out from among the trees. He saw her at once and rode briskly over.

"Miss Bradford?" He made it a question.

She nodded.

"I've got a message for you."

Sandra waited. The young man, sitting a sorrel mare, seemed disconcerted by her direct stare. She had not meant to be rude. She was only surprised.

"Yes?" she encouraged him.

He tipped back his hat, ran his fingers down the front of his checked shirt, then fingered his belt buckle.

After a self-conscious cough he said, "Dr. Pelham said you're to wait here. Help will be coming in the morning."

He wheeled the sorrel and would have gone off, except Sandra called after him. "What kind of help?"

"He didn't say," the youth said, sitting high with reins held as if ready to take off once again.

"Wouldn't you like to rest?" Sandra asked.

"I sure would," but pointing toward the setting sun, "except I'd better get out of here while I can still find my way."

"Would you tell Dr. Pelham thanks?" Sandra asked.

"If I see him."

"Good-bye," Sandra said.

"Good-bye," the boy said, wheeling the horse. Then he abruptly reined the horse in again, and turning to her, said, "You're going to be on television tonight." Then at a brisk trot he and the horse disappeared among the trees.

Television, Sandra thought. Well, that explained the helicopter.

Raising up, Sandra looked to where the boy and the horse had disappeared among the trees. She found it hard to believe he had come and was gone, and then when she lay back down her mind rattled through door after door of reflection and speculation before sleep mercifully turned the keys on all the doors.

30

Twice she was awakened during the night by screams from Rimrock and Cossack. Rimrock's nuptial victory in coupling with Brandy had done more than whet his appetite for further possible conquests. It had also, it seemed, so boosted his own estimate of his abilities as a herd stallion that the time had come when he could no longer be driven off to run the periphery of the herd slavering for the mares Cossack claimed as his.

Sandra had known that time might arrive, and having witnessed a few fights, feared for both horses, unless the white stallion in a quickly decisive flurry of teeth and hooves could convince Rimrock to await for another time, when the white stallion would be older and weaker, and he, Rimrock, even larger and stronger.

Stallion confrontations were by no means the rule among the wild ones. Usually the outcast stallion only stayed in waiting, avoiding a direct confrontation with the herd stud. Then would come busy times and one or another impatient mare would peel off from the herd, and so, in time, by waiting — and sometimes pilfering — the patient stallion soon had a herd of his own and he'd break away to sire his own dynasty.

When daylight finally began to ooze down into the clearing Sandra lifted herself to survey the herd. Counting heads, she determined all were there, and getting up she went among the trees briefly, and then came down to the sump, which was now filled with clear water.

Bending to wash her face she got a quick, distorted view of herself and was shocked by the sight, the welts left by whip snaps of branches across her face, dark sockets holding her eyes, her hair a tangled bird's nest decorated with pine needles and twigs.

She was, she told herself, a mess. Her denims and shirt were torn in a dozen places, and both were caked with mud from the sump. Her fingernails were broken, ragged. Running a tongue along her upper lip she could taste grit. The dirt was ground into her wrists, into the palms of her hands. Even after she washed them they came back out of the water still gray with dirt.

Well, if nothing else, this had to be clean-up day. She could even smell herself, so breakfast could wait. Undressing on the spot, she crawled into the sump hole and with her last sliver of soap began the job of lathering her body in the resistant, slightly sulfurous water.

Lathered and rinsed once, she reached for her clothes and began to wash them. The cleansing ritual lasted an hour, and when at last she stepped from the sump hole she couldn't help but wonder how the horses would like the water after she'd fouled it with soap.

Back at camp, which was what she called the area around Brandy's saddle, she put on her boots and kicked apart a pine stump. Wood from its resinous heart flared quickly and she hung her clothes on bending sticks to dry. Digging out a brush from the duffel, she stood so close the fire singed her legs while she brushed and braided her hair.

She put the clothes back on while still damp, and stood by the fire to dry them on her body. Then she looked to breakfast — eight dates, one candy bar, and a tiny can of Spam.

Looking out across the clearing she saw Cossack had come to the sump to drink. He lowered his head and then raised and tossed it in bewilderment. Undeterred, however, he lowered it again and drank.

Meanwhile, nearly two hundred yards up the incline, Sandra saw Rimrock edging sideways in a coy little canter toward the mare. And this time the mare did not switch ends, but stood waiting.

Perhaps Cossack was instinctively aware of the mare's sudden acquiescence, or perhaps out of the sides of his big eyes, he saw it happen.

At any rate he wheeled away from the water and with a tremendous surge of power went charging up the hill to where Rimrock was preparing to mount his conquest.

Cossack hit Rimrock broadside with both front hooves just as he was raising himself to accommodate the mare. Off balance, the red horse went crashing to the ground, the wind knocked out of him.

Cossack screamed as he backed off for yet another charging assault. Startled, the mare fled a little way and then turned to watch complacently and await the victor. Rimrock staggered to his feet as Cossack hit him another glancing blow across the withers.

The second blow sent him stumbling down the incline with the white stallion in pursuit. When Cossack bit his flank, Rimrock tried to present the white stallion with a set of hoofprints for his chest, but still gasping for air, the effort fell short.

Cossack could have stopped then, turned back to the mare. The fight was over. He had his enemy in full retreat. There was no need for more fighting.

But the white stallion seemed out for blood. Screaming again and again he lashed out with hooves and teeth until Rimrock was in full, blinding flight, galloping madly down the incline between the charred stumps, through the new green brush of rebirth.

Sandra stood petrified at Cossack's savagery. This was a horse determined to kill. This was a horse driven by more than the usual instincts of stallion dominance, a horse who had learned to hate.

But Rimrock, having regained his wind, was gaining on the white stallion, and gradually Sandra's breathing returned to normal, her fists unclenched.

Then it happened. Rimrock tripped, went to his knees, slid along the ground with outstretched neck, and then his huge body somersaulted and came down with a crash.

The fall must have so astounded Cossack he went running right on by, and then slowing, he circled quickly to come back up the hill to where the mare was waiting.

Sandra ran stumbling through the brush to where the red stallion lay. His eyes were rolling wildly. Froth coated his muzzle, outlined his nostrils, and sweat streaked his withers, his chest.

She bent over. His halter had hooked under an old pine root. She knew instantly and without question that the sudden, savage, twisting somersault had broken his back.

It happened often enough. Cattle coming blindly to somersault over wire. Horses being flipped by a prairie-dog hole. She had seen enough such casualties not to know.

Quickly she undid the halter. Rimrock managed to roll over on his belly. He managed to paw the earth with his front hooves. But from the withers back there was nothing, not even a quiver to indicate that a miracle had perhaps saved one nerve, one muscle.

Time and again the big red horse tried to lift, to drag himself with his front hooves, and the horror in his eyes was the horror of the rabbit as the horned owl's talons break its spine.

Sandra knelt by his head as if to comfort him, but he tossed his head so wildly she was thrown clear.

"Red, Red . . .," she started to beg. And then the stallion screamed, and she put her hands over her ears and turned away.

At first she walked slowly as a woman who has just seen a child killed by a car — numb, confused. Then she quickened her pace until at last she was running.

In camp she pulled the rifle from the scabbard, and then she went slowly back down the incline to where the great horse lay.

He had stopped struggling now, but his head was still high and his eyes were bright with the agony of a horse who will never again run with the wind. He watched Sandra approach, and made one feeble attempt to raise his body with the power in his front legs. Sandra thought she saw acceptance, or maybe it was only that she wanted to believe that her horse would forgive her this thing she had to do.

Only once did she hesitate. When she was twenty feet away she paused, groped with her mind for some alternative, little matter how tenuous such a thread of hope.

But there was none, and so she squeezed her eyelids tight to free her eyes of tears, and walking to within five feet of the stallion's head, she cocked the rifle and, aiming, heard the roar of his death.

She levered another shell into the chamber and shot again. Levered still another and once more pulled the trigger.

Then before his eyes began to glaze, she turned and walked up the slope and leaned the gun against a tree stump.

Sitting with her back to the saddle, her mind was clear, her nerves steady, and she could think coherently.

She thought as she sat there that she would have liked to bury him, to save him from the buzzards. And then unpredictably some small thought said, "But why underground, food for only the worms?"

Why not let his body feed the birds which soar so high and so free? Why not the little fox or the clever coyote? Why not the furred and the feathered ones instead of the crawling worms?

Maybe there was even some glory in returning to earth on broad wings and padding feet instead of taking the slimy route through a worm's belly.

So absorbed had she been by these strange thoughts, her mind had ignored the warning whinnies of the horse herd. When finally the nickering pierced the traumatic curtain which threatened to shadow her mind, she looked up to see riders emerging from among the trees.

Riders on horses and on mules, and even one small rider on a burro. Twenty, then thirty . . . she couldn't count how many, coming slowly, carefully, so as not to spook the wild herd, across the big burn.

Dr. Pelham's promise was being kept.

31

When the riders had cleared the trees, a sun-tanned man wearing a black beret and sitting high in the saddle rode over to her.

"Good morning," he said. She returned the greeting. "We heard shooting."

"A broken back," Sandra said. "The stallions were fighting." She didn't tell him that the dead horse belonged to her.

"It happens," the man said, and then added, "My name is Roy Coldagelli. I am one of the owners of the vineyards. We have heard of your heroic attempts to save the wild horses. We want to help. We have cleared a way across the valley, a route to the Rantan Reservation."

The man's voice was low, comforting. Sandra didn't know what to say. She was afraid she might weep. "It must have been a most arduous journey," he continued. "We would like you to finish it in safety."

A few tears did escape and rolled down Sandra's cheeks. The man went on as though he hadn't seen them: "How are the horses? Can they be driven?"

"I've been with them a long time," Sandra said, composing herself. "They are accustomed to being herded. I think we could do it."

The man smiled. "That will make it easier," he said, "because as you can see, my companions aren't exactly cowboys. Matter of fact, some have difficulty just staying in the saddle. They are my workers. Then there are also other grape growers, owners of neighboring vineyards. There are villagers too, and some vegetable growers . . . they are not horsemen, but they are willing."

Sandra smiled. "You . . . they are very generous."

"No," the man said, "it is you who are generous. We too want to see the wild horses safe on the Rantan Reservation. We too hate the horse killers." He hesitated, then asked, "Since you are undoubtedly the most experienced horse person here, maybe you have a suggestion about how this drive might be accomplished."

Sandra looked at the scuffed toes of her riding boots, and then back up at the man. "How many riders do you have?" she asked.

"Perhaps forty. Maybe closer to fifty."

"I think we should surround the herd, surround the clearing with riders, and then very slowly converge on the horses, and holding a close semicircle bring them down to the valley."

"It sounds like it might work."

"Most important," Sandra said, "is to walk the horses. No rider should push his horse beyond a walk. We can't afford to panic the herd, to let them run. I think if one does run, we should just let him. If he slips through the cordon, then we should let him go. We can always come back and pick him up with a rope."

"Sounds like a most excellent maneuver. Shall we start?"

"Soon as I catch my horse and get her saddled."

"Good. Meanwhile I will go back to my friends and explain it all to them. They are anxious to help. There are many more people anxious to help, and they are waiting in the valley. They all heard about you and the horses last night on television, radio, and in the newspapers. They think you are doing something good."

Dr. Pelham again, Sandra thought. That bearded saint of a summertime recluse had masterminded a public relations coup slick enough to make a Madison Avenue publicist envious.

It turned out Coldagelli had an equally fantastic talent for explaining clearly, plainly, and precisely what was expected of each rider, and they disappeared among the trees one by one in single file.

When only Coldagelli was left in the clearing, she got out the map to make a last entry:

"Fifteenth day. July 12. Rimrock is dead. Strangely I feel no great sorrow. Maybe it's because the herd has become more important than just one horse."

Then she mounted, and with what little gear she had left secured behind her saddle, Sandra waited. A half hour passed, and the horses the man and the girl were sitting began fidgeting. Finally Coldagelli put his fingers to his lips and whistled shrilly.

One by one the riders began to emerge from the trees on all sides of the clearing, and always closing their formation they moved cautiously to form a horseshoe of resistance around the wild horse herd.

Just as slowly and cautiously the wild ones began to drift ahead of the riders.

It was a perfect maneuver. Grandma took the direction within minutes, and Cossack and his latest love brought up the rear.

When the wild horses reached the fringe of trees they hesitated, but only for a moment. Then they moved on. Now, among the trees, the riders called softly to one another to keep their formation, and not a wild one bolted, nor did any rider lose his complacency, and within an hour the band of horses was out from beneath the high pines onto the grassy floor of the valley.

Sandra's heart seemed to jump and almost stick in her throat when she saw the crowds waiting at the entrance to a vineyard road. All kinds of people had formed a huge human funnel into which the wild ones might literally be poured. After the first quick murmur of excitement which seemed to rise from a hundred spasmodic whispers, they were silent — silent as the sun.

The sights and smells were at first too much for the wild horses. They turned to charge back toward the riders. But the riders had by then formed a solid wall of horseflesh, and the band turned and galloped back toward the funnel of waiting people.

Coldagelli whistled. The riders halted their mounts. Then for fifteen minutes the mustangs raced around in the corral formed by human pickets. Gradually they quieted, gathered in a milling circle, and then Grandma took the first tentative step toward the break in the ranks, the point at which the human corral funneled out onto the road.

Step by wary step she approached the only way out of what she surely must have considered a trap. Step by step the rest of the herd followed. Then with a short burst of speed she was on the road between the rows of grapevines and after a brief run she slowed to a walk, and all the riders closed in behind the herd.

At every crossroads there was a human barricade. Where the parade passed adobe houses, low barns, entrances to brick wine cellars, the winery buildings . . . people stood watching. And if a horse skittered at the sudden flutter of a skirt or a white handkerchief, or started to run because of childish laughter . . . all quickly broke stride and followed Grandma's placid pace.

Such a march as the horses were making would never have succeeded with elk or deer or antelope. They would have panicked, broken through the rows of people, leaped over their heads. But these were feral horses, descendants of a breed long subservient to man, and already a girl had brought them a long, long way.

Sandra was hardly aware of the passage of time. Riding beside Coldagelli to lead the long lines of pseudo-cowboys, she had the feeling she was herding dynamite and at any moment it might explode. She watched Grandma's ears for signs of trouble. She kept a sharp eye on Cossack, hoping he wouldn't go left or right in a berserk gamble for freedom, pulling the rest of the herd into a stampede which might trample right over the fence line of people.

And then quite suddenly they were free from the miles and miles of grapes, along a dusty road, and on either side there was a woven wire fence, and for the first time Sandra felt the muscles in her neck relax.

"Hardly four miles now," Coldagelli said. "Maybe less."

But Sandra did not hear him, because there among the people crowded along the roadway was her father, the ranch hands, and even Mrs. Webley. They were waving, and she waved back, and her father stopped smiling long enough to shout, "Sandy! Sandy!"

Television cameras mounted on trucks which had been waiting on down the road began creeping closer to the marching horses. Coldagelli rose in his saddle to gesture them back.

"Inside the range!" he shouted. "There'll be plenty of time when we're on the preserve."

In a surprisingly short time the high archway

marking the preserve came into view. For a brief moment then there was time to think of Rimrock and be sad, but quickly Sandra took solace in the hope that next summer Brandy would present her with a red colt that looked like the dead stallion.

Now Coldagelli's horse increased the pace, broke from a walk into a canter, and the riders behind, glad to be moving, began to shout.

Grandma took the cue and began to gallop. The horses raced forward until they were pressing Brandy's flanks. The crowd cheered as Sandra joined the wild rush. Standing beside the archway was Dr. Pelham, an impish grin parting his white beard. She had done it. It was over, and it was not hard to say good-bye to the wild horse herd because now she would have the satisfaction of knowing they were safe.

In a clatter of pounding hooves the horses swept past in a cloud of dust and were free among the tall grasses of the Rantan Reservation.